Hina Belitz grew up in Ando author and renowned equal r in law and creative writing from Brunel and Cambridge University respectively. Her debut novel, SET ME FREE, was critically acclaimed and led to her being interviewed by Morgan Freeman to star in a National Geographic documentary about love. She lives in Hertfordshire with her husband and two sons and her writing has appeared in numerous publications including the *Guardian* and the BBC online.

Praise for Hina Belitz:

'Genuinely funny scenes' *Cosmopolitan*

'Poignant . . . Will transport you lock, stock and barrel to another place' *Trip Fiction*

'Read, loved and highly recommended' *Tamworth Book Club*

'A deeply moving, quietly powerful story . . . empowering and inspiring' *The Herald*

'[A] moving tale' *Marie Claire*

*By Hina Belitz*

Set Me Free
To Lahore, With Love

# To Lahore, With Love

## HINA BELITZ

REVIEW

First published in Great Britain in paperback in 2020 by
Headline Review
An imprint of HEADLINE PUBLISHING GROUP

1

Cataloguing in Publication Data is available from the British Library

ISBN 978 1 4722 3173 4

Typeset in Sabon by Avon DataSet Ltd, Bidford-on-Avon, Warwickshire

Printed and bound by Clays Ltd, Elcograf S.p.A.

HEADLINE PUBLISHING GROUP
An Hachette UK Company
Carmelite House
50 Victoria Embankment
London EC4Y 0DZ

www.headline.co.uk
www.hachette.co.uk

For my mother and grandmother,
awe-inspiring matriarchs and immensely
talented cooks.


And for Zak and Haris, always.

My formula for greatness in a human being is
*amor fati*: that one wants nothing to be different,
not forward, not backward, not in all eternity.
Not merely bear what is necessary, still less
conceal it . . . but love it

Friedrich Nietzsche

# Contents

The page numbers that follow the recipe headings are a reference to the cookery book *MS MAYFORD'S RECIPES TO CHANGE YOUR LIFE: A MANUAL OF ART AND SCIENCE TO CHANGE HEARTS AND MINDS WITH DELICIOUS DISHES; YOUR MENTAL HEALTH COMPANION AND DAY BOOK OF ARTFUL ENDEAVOURS.*

# Prologue

THERE IS SOMETHING DIFFERENT, UNFAMILIAR IN THE entrance hall. She breathes in slow and deep as she closes the front door behind her. The scent of earth, equal parts musk and saline, rides above the familiar notes: ribbons of air freshener, traces of an earlier meal, Gabe's particular smell still hanging ever-present in the air like a promise. And his scent is strong, stronger than usual. She places her shopping, the ingredients for this evening's meal, on the kitchen worktop, ever so quietly. Christ Church clock framed in their kitchen window says it's 6.00pm. Gabe will still be at work. She's planned a special meal tonight, a dish to elicit amorous inclinations, this being her ovulation 'time of the month'. One of her three fertile days for scheduled lovemaking. She dismisses her misgivings and strikes a match to light the stove. It's a moment she loves, a rite of passage to her mysterious world of cookery. She is hypnotised by that explosive moment before the ebb and sway of flame.

She draws back. Something is still troubling her. She waves out the flame and sniffs like a tracker dog, sensing something beyond the char of snuffed match. It's there. That spectre of human presence: warmth, moisture, the disturbance of air. She knows she's not alone. In the hall, the line of wedding photos to her right, stairs to her left, she hears it: the creak of floorboard upstairs. A familiar sound she recognises as the spot at the end of their bed, the spot they avoid if they rise at night.

*Someone is upstairs.*

Gabe, she thinks, but it can't be. He's still at work. She considers. Should she call out? Something stops her. She takes one stair at a time, breaking between to gather nerve. The silence is dense and full, like a breath held in. That unfamiliar scent lingers in pockets here and there. The top step creaks.

'Who's there . . . Addy?' a voice says. It's her Gabe, his pitch higher than usual.

She releases her trapped breath in a long slow stream, goes limp with relief. 'Gabe. What are you doing home?' she says, stepping into the bedroom.

And that's when it hits, at once, thick as a wall.

She gags at the warm fug of cheap floral perfume and curdled sweat. Gabe's in bed. It's not his familiar sprawl, arms and legs akimbo, sheets in a mess. He's propped on his elbows, rigid, limbs aligned, sheets pulled up to his neck like a child in hiding, pretending he's not there. There's no move to welcome her, none of his usual lifting of the sheets to invite her in.

'Why are you home so early? . . . And in bed,' she says, voicing thoughts more than questions. Her hand strokes her belly.

'I'm sick, Ads. Some fluey thing.'

*Liar!* He is flushed but there's no weight of fever on his eyes.

'You should have phoned,' he says. 'Weren't you supposed to be out tonight?'

*Why would I call?*

She scans the room without answering. Beside him, her pillow lies punched in an unfamiliar way. Dented, so it's half inside itself like a cup fallen on its side. As she steps forward, the scents strengthen. Salt, damp leaves, sweat. Her neck begins to tingle. The same feeling when her cookery is going well. The feeling that tells her that her instincts are right.

The wardrobe door is ajar, but the clothes she'd left in a spill that morning are gone. Then something catches her eye behind the frosted glass panel of the wardrobe door. A shift so slight you could persuade yourself you didn't see it. But she is certain she did. For a moment she holds it in. The fury and shame. The humiliation and hurt. All that is about to unfold. A scene enters her head,

3

one imagined a thousand and one times: *caught red-handed*. She takes a small step forward. Towards the wardrobe. And then one more. Next, three intentional strides.

She sees Gabe's knuckles whiten as his fists tighten.

'Addy,' he says, his voice urgent. 'Addy.' Louder now.

In a moment she's there by the wardrobe, her breath jagged. His voice reaches her as if in a tunnel.

'Shall we go downstairs?' he says. 'Have some tea?'

She reaches out, her hand now resting on the wardrobe door. She leaves it there. Enjoys the power.

There is a sliver of a gap. From it, the ooze of sweat. A thread of cocoa butter. She can almost feel the woman's heart beating on the other side of the wardrobe door.

She grips the knob so hard the cold metal hurts.

'Addy,' he says. 'Addy.'

She tightens her grip, her fingers white, bloodless.

Then she pushes the door closed.

A reassuring click.

Lies. Deceit. Hurt. Locked away and hidden.

He is shocked. His jaw loose, lips apart.

And she knows.

After a beat, she looks at him square on.

'Tea,' she says, turning to leave. 'I'll nip out for milk.'

# BEFORE

# 1

# Commitment Cake (*page 9*)

For love and tenderness, the kind that leads to commitment, take:

260g butter, melted and warm
200g sugar
500g semolina
300g yogurt, made foamy and quivering by stirring in 1 tbsp baking powder
1 lemon or lime, juice only
300g sugar, dissolved in 200ml water
1 tbsp orange blossom water for the attar glaze

The *taste*: sweet, buttery and floral but with bite. These flavours will surprise you.
The *artistry*: the power of the meeting of East and West.
The *purpose*: to introduce unfamiliar tastes through the familiar vessel of cake so the taster becomes open to that which they may not otherwise accept.

TWO YEARS AGO, I WAS GETTING READY FOR THE MOST important evening of my life. It was an overcast mid-October day in London and I was eighteen years old. *This is the day my life begins*, I told myself. It felt as if everything that had come before had been to prepare me for this moment, the moment Gabe proposed. As it happened, I was entirely wrong.

That night I wore black eyeliner with an upward sweep, which suits the almond shape of my dark eyes, and hair piled high with diamante pins. I needed a good few because even though I have my mother's pale Irish skin, I also inherited my father's thick Asian hair. I chose a little black dress (of course) combined with one of Nana's sequined scarves. When people ask me where I'm from – receptionists, shopkeepers – I reply, 'Where do you think?' or often, if I'm feeling tired, 'London,' knowing that's not what they mean. They're really asking about my parentage. I've long known my looks confuse people.

The evening started with a Commitment Cake I'd prepared earlier and brought over to Gabe's. As long as I can remember, I'd liked nothing better than to cook. You could say I was obsessed. I was currently working as an apprentice chef at a local eatery called Arabian Delights but dreamed one day of setting up my own kitchen or even working at some famous Michelin-starred restaurant.

It is unconventional to start an evening meal with dessert, but not if you have experienced the scent and taste of this dish. The taste of everlasting love. I busied myself in Gabe's kitchen, heating up the cake and completing the preparation. As it emerged from the oven, I set it before him on the dining table, moistening a pinch of it with a dewy attar glaze, the scent of orange blossom laced with caramel and lime, then raising it for him to take a bite. I purposefully missed his mouth a little, so he was forced to lick his lips. His eyes rolled up in his head as he turned the flavours around in his mouth and then he released such a forceful moan you'd be forgiven for mistaking it for pain. It was a total success. But then as I started preparations for the rest of the evening meal, he shuffled me out of his house.

\* \* \*

We end up at this toff's restaurant, one we can't really afford, and I start moaning about the meal – pasta beyond al dente, no hint of truffle in the *tagliatelle al tartufo bianco d'Alba*, and most telling of all, onions diced instead of sliced. We don't normally eat out, due to my obsession with cookery, but Gabe had insisted. He has a confident way about him that makes people do as he says. Moving the subject away from my disappointing pasta, I say, 'Talk to me about physics, Gabe.' I always love it when he talks science at me. He weaves his fingertips into an apex, then does that motionless stare of an academic deep in thought, the kind that brings heat to my face.

Somewhere behind me I hear an old Spandau Ballet song Mum loves. *Oh, I want the truth to be said*, it bemoans, a ringtone which abruptly cuts off.

Gabe says, 'It's the study of what's real, Ads. We live in a universe so big that no human mind can comprehend it. There's this massive force holding it all together in the endless dark' – he sweeps the air – 'but we can't see it, hear it, smell it, taste or touch it. We don't know anything about it and like all things we wish to know, we name it.'

(I pout the letter G before I realise the question is rhetorical.)

'Dark energy,' he announces. 'So,' he says, looking about the room as if following the trail of a fly, 'here we are amongst billions of suns and planets, alone. Tiny beings balancing on the dry crusts of a wet planet in a corner of this endless expanse, observing, measuring. And all this is out there, Ads.' He takes my hand and says, with the slightest tremor on his lips, 'Yet since we met, I can think only of you.'

It is the happiest day of my life. Not because of his Addy versus the universe compliment, that I am tested against the very universe and win, or because he follows it with a proposal of marriage. But because it is then that I know my plan has worked: my plan to *make* him fall in love with me. I, Addy Mayford, chef extraordinaire, magician of food, have cooked up his love. Literally. Each dish – its taste, scent, sizzle, texture, colour, and my very own dark energy, the invisible power of intention I fry, bake and knead into every bite – has brought Gabe to this moment. Him loving me.

As we left the restaurant, hands clasped, I cast my eyes up to the night sky, the stars bright points of light breaking through the dark. I remember the feeling of heat, light and electricity; the effervescent elation which shortened my breath and sent unsettling tingles to my toes. In the restaurant, I had responded to Gabe's proposal with a smile, nothing more.

On the street he walks me back against a wall, his eyes devouring me. Tracing the curve of my lips, my jaw, my neck with his fingertip, he says it again. 'Marry me, Addy.' I smile, say nothing. And then, placing my palm on his cheek, 'Perhaps,' I say, my tone nonchalant as I enjoy my superhero powers over him. He takes my hand and kisses the centre of my palm. Inside, every part of me is screaming *Yes!* and *Thank you, Lord! Thank you, Commitment Cake!* for I am in no doubt I owe it to the special recipes I'd prepared with empirical precision.

Since then, I have come to better understand matters of the heart and the many reasons we choose to marry. Whatever the reason, whether it's money, good looks, security, one thing is certain: we all marry for love. It's just we all love different things; and not only the person we are marrying.

And I was no exception – I just didn't realise it back then.

Of course, by the time we'd reached my home, I'd said yes. Yes, yes, yes!

I grew up in the kitchen of our red-brick mid-terrace house in East London, because that's where Nana spent all her time. I started cooking with Nana from the moment I could stand, first by helping spoon ingredients into pans and later preparing entire meals like a virtuoso. Cookery was the most important activity in our lives.

But there was more to it than that.

Nana's recipes had powers beyond the marvel of human sustenance. The recipes handed down to her through generation upon generation of mothers could cure any emotionally delicate state or ill mood. Like the time I returned bullied and bruised from school, when Unpleasantness-Cancelling Lentils fixed my smarting and hurt heart. Or when I was overtaken with examination fears and Stay Cool Yogurt Dumplings settled my nerves as if I'd just returned from holiday.

And more still. There were recipes that we believed could actually *change* people, guaranteeing a desired outcome as reliably as those unbreakable laws of nature. They worked. Every time. And so I fried and dried and glazed and boiled to fulfil my particular aims. Food became my vocabulary, so where others used words and sentences to express or persuade, I used the power of taste and the curved satisfaction of a full belly. A calming Cloud Lentil to build resolve to face a thorny dilemma, a Brave Chilli Chicken for courage to accept a challenge, or a Red Rice Soup to soothe a troubled mind. But the thing is, most people don't believe in such things, even if they work. And why should they? They haven't seen what my Nana's diced lamb and cauliflower can do, or her butter maple flatbreads. *Wah!*

From our kitchen window in Spitalfields, brilliant sunshine would be magnified by the angular white walls of Christ Church. Its clock face, set on a single tall steeple above its entrance, gave it the look of some sphinx-like creature on its haunches watching over me. It would watch as I sat cross-legged under the table, dangled my legs on the worktop, crouched on the floor gazing into the oven, or stood on a chair staring into Nana's bubbling pans. I liked nothing better than cooking with Nana. Countless times as a baby, I'd narrowly escaped death by fire with my Moses basket practically butt up against flaming cooking pots. At least that's what Mum would say. And when Mum would complain, on the few occasions she wasn't working, Nana'd just say, 'Eh! Stop your *buk-buk* . . . tsk.'

I was raised by a Catholic mother of Irish extraction and a Muslim grandmother from Pakistan under the same roof, both handing me back and forth as if I were two separate people, each never making reference to the perfectly circular world of the other. So, church service on Sunday followed mosque on Friday for *Jumma* prayers; confession followed a group *Dhikr* remembrance of God; a rosary of Hail Marys followed tasbih-bead recitation of the ninety-nine names of God; styled hair followed headscarves. And so it went. Over the years I came to consider myself neither fully Christian nor completely Muslim, being more a fusion of the two – a Mustian or Chrislim, I'd tell Jen, my best friend, chuckling as I mouthed the portmanteau. (*But that's not a religion*, she'd reply. Jen's not the brightest.) Whether Christian, Muslim, agnostic or atheist, one thing was certain: I was at all times and without exception a devout chef. My religiosity in the conventional sense had fissures in a way my commitment to cookery did not. When I was cooking, there would be no such laxity. My cookery was precise and controlled while at the same time being artistic and expressive, sponges rising to even perfection, onions browned as if by an artist's brush. And I was an artist on a mission, which, as with all art, was to affect a permanent change in those who interacted with it. Cookery was to me like faith itself.

My Nana had been a legendary beauty (her words), so beautiful she would draw a crowd whenever she left the house (also her words). This she told me as I gazed upon her tan-leather-coloured skin and halo-white hair. I would try to picture Nana as young, but I never could. She'd always looked old, a little witch-like with her grooved skin and Roman nose. Even in my earliest memories, I cannot remember a time she looked any different. It was as if she didn't age.

Nana had grown up in North Pakistan, where she said you could see lush green meadows and clouds pouring over high mountains. For the Yousafzai tribe, Nana's tribe, the given name of a child and what it means is a matter of great importance, said to influence the child's personality. As a young girl, I never thought of her as having a name other than Nana, but in later years I came to know that her actual name was Asiyah. She loved it because her namesake was considered one of the greatest women in history. Asiyah received this accolade for standing up to her husband, a brutal pharaoh who reigned at the time of Moses, when he insisted she worship him as God. She died in the name of her cause. Since hearing this, I've often pondered: are women destined to forever suffer at the hands of men? Nana was proud of her name, although she had wondered if that was the reason she had ended up marrying an arrogant pharaonic loser who had left her, mainly because when he struck her at will for some trivial concern, Nana deployed the retaliatory maxim 'an eye for an eye', and struck him right back. But there had never been any hope for her marriage. It was a wonder it lasted as long as it did, bringing into the world my Aunty Gulu, Uncle Musa and my father.

Unfazed by the disappointments of her life, Nana had decided her future lay with her younger son. And so she moved to the UK to be with him around twenty years ago when he married Mum. Mum said Nana arrived wearing a shimmering sky-blue sari in some diaphanous material, layers of which were quivering over her Dr Martens-shaped boots. Everyone made way for her without question, because that's what you did in her presence.

The thing I loved best about my Nana's kitchen was the big black pestle and mortar we'd had for as long as I could remember. Its bowl base was rough-cut black stone, deep and wide, and the pestle was a long wooden club which reminded me of a baseball bat. It had the look of a dark, rough boulder sat there on our kitchen worktop, even when it was being used to pound herbs and spices for our evening meal. Nana told me it had been a bargain because the stonemason who'd made it had slipped, chipping its perfect upper edge. But that was what I loved best about it. I would run my fingers around the rim, feeling the ellipse and the sharp indentation where the maker had slipped. It was a witness mark. Proof of hands at labour; that it hadn't been churned out of some factory. She would tell me of the many weeks it would take to make a single one, of the tap-a-tap rhythms at Urdu Bazaar where she'd bought it, and how no two pestle and mortars could ever be the same. Like the soul. And how after so many hours of sweaty hammering and shaping, one slip, like a misdeed, could ruin the whole thing. I think she saw it as a metaphor for life.

Everything for Nana had deeper meaning, even mundane things you wouldn't give a second thought to. Events you'd see as chance, such as the wrong turn at a junction, a spoiled meal, an unexpected visitor . . . for Nana, they happened for a reason. There were messages everywhere – hidden in the shape of steam issuing from a broth, in the scent of first rain on parched earth, the patterns the sun drew on our walls through our netted panes. Our lives were full of mystery and magic in that way; the possibility of the impossible was always there at the edges. It gave Nana a visionary quality, like an oracle or fortune teller, as she went around the house mouthing prayers in a whisper on the beads of her tasbih. And that's the way I think of her. Wise old Nana who was partly here and partly in some ephemeral plane, a momentary unseen world only she could perceive, separated from ours by the finest of veils. That's perhaps why she knew things she shouldn't know. Like her visionary dream of me marrying an angel, just before I met Gabriel, a name shared in the Abrahamic tradition with the highest-ranking angel of them all. We didn't think it strange, though. That was just Nana.

Nana was also a feeder. Feeding others was in her DNA (and consequently in mine). She would feed anyone and everyone who came within a few metres of our home. Neighbours were frequently plied with Nana's latest creation. She even fed the haters. Like old Mr Jenkins, with monastic tonsured hair, who'd come to complain about the cookery smells, his face a knot of anger; after a bowl of Lose Your Anger Chicken and a big cup of tea, he left full-bellied, a baggy grin on his face. 'It's important to feed your foes,' Nana said after he left, 'because it may just loosen their hate.' Then Mrs Dennison from three doors away, a permanently bitter witch of a lady greatly versed in the art of spite. She had great eye bags with, I was certain, actual space for the storage of small items. She never stopped cursing: endless venomous tirades about her husband, her kids, the weather, the price of groceries. Nana softened her with a Hate-Melting Haleem Stew and a sweet and crispy flat bread paratha oozing melted butter and maple syrup. She didn't speak for a full twenty minutes, and although her new expression couldn't be described as a smile, the scowl had definitely lifted. She came every week to eat with us after that.

When I cast my mind back, I see that Nana was in so many ways like a living calamine balm. It wasn't just the soothing and healing effect of her cookery; there were also the stories. Nana always said stories are guardians of wisdom, and that folded within them are great truths. Every night, we would enter this dark world populated by mystical characters and otherworldly creatures and with them she would work magic. Sometimes the stories were about luminaries like Abraham, Joseph or Jesus, religious figures who were subjected to great trials. How I loved to hear Nana's stories.

It was only when I'd bring up Dad, saying something along the lines of, 'Dad would have loved this story,' that her flow faltered and her eyes dropped. Time for bed, she would say, even when it wasn't. He was the 'elephant in the room' of our little family. Neither Nana or Mum would mention him. No one would, except me.

It was probably because he'd left us.

Or perhaps because now he was dead.

They never said.

# 2

# Happy-Making Muffins (*page 11*)

For difference and otherness to combine and create
something truly beautiful, take:

250g unsalted butter, melted
250g sugar
350g plain flour
300g walnuts, coarsely chopped
pinch sea salt
pinch baking powder
2 large eggs
1 large onion, blended

The taste: savoury and sweet.
The artistry: the tension created from the meeting of
vastly different elements, leading the whole to become
more than the sum of its parts.
The purpose: to bring joy and connection beyond expectation.

WE'D ALWAYS LIVED TOGETHER, THREE GENERATIONS OF females under one roof. My care after Dad left had been a deal between Nana and Mum. Both agreed to have equal parts in my upbringing and to never question the way the other chose to raise me, as long as there was no mention of Dad. Mum would come and go. She preferred absence to presence after Dad and was often away working: different locations, different towns and even different countries at times. Sometimes we would see her when she came home, other times not. She'd go to bed and not emerge. Later, sometimes after a whole day, she would reappear. For Nana and me, it was the same whether Mum was home or away. We would take a meal to her in her bedroom, loading it with a weight of wishes that she might become happy again. It seemed to work, but then, so soon, she'd hug me and be gone again becoming as distant and downcast as before. That was how life went.

Despite this, my upbringing was a very happy one. I was well loved, and Mum and Nana were enough. At least that's what I told myself. But, in truth, I felt a sense of something missing after Dad left. I, like any child with an absent parent, harboured a secret fantasy that one day he would return to us and everything would be wonderful again. I would imagine dappled sunshine over a ferny forest floor, a weave of branches above us as Mum, Nana, Dad and I walked between trees to a meadow of long grass and wild flowers, a bit like a scene from a Disney movie. It was an elaborate fantasy. Of course, this never happened, and soon the dreams diminished until they faded to nothing more than a hole where Dad used to be. I was fine, though. I wanted for nothing. Really.

But then Dad died.

It happened just a few months after he'd left, shortly after my seventh birthday party. Mum sat me down on the sofa and clasped me in one of her trademark endless hugs.

'Addy,' she said. 'You're a strong girl, aren't you, pet?'

'Yes, Mum,' I said, knowing from her voice that something bad was to follow.

I wept silent tears as Mum rocked me back and forth. She told me that it had happened in Lahore, where Dad had lived after he left us, and that it had something to do with a road incident involving a motorbike and a donkey. I shouldn't have cared. Hadn't he walked out on us anyway? But I did.

Nana, who was downcast but composed with a tightness about her face, then carried out a ritual which afterwards became customary whenever something bad happened. First, she reached up to the high shelf below which the small replica of a grandfather clock hung and brought down a swaddled book. The wrapping was tapered, and very gently, first pulling her head covering properly over her hair, she teased open the binding and unravelled the fabric which had been wrapped so many times around the book that it looked like something mummified by the Egyptians. As she unwrapped it, starting with a string-like slither, the fabric grew wider and wider until it assumed the width of the book, ending in a tailored pocket. With great reverence, she lifted the book from its pouch, the swaddling left heaped on the table like the cast-off of a pretend ghost, and raised it to her lips to kiss the cover and then touch it upon her forehead, repeating this three times before opening the book at random. It was the Quran, the holy book of Islam. Her forefinger ran, right to left, down the page, following line by line the curvaceous letters which swooped and danced along it. She read silently, as I'd seen her do before, her mouth whispering, her lips animated. I remember marvelling at these strange unreadable marks, so full of mystery. When she was done, she stroked me on my head, her eyes heavy with concern for my sadness.

Next was a story in which a great challenge was overcome: the tale of the child sage for whom the flames into which he'd been thrown had miraculously cooled when he cried out the special words, *God is sufficient and the best disposer of affairs.* It was normal to borrow the prayerful words of the great sages and prophets of the past, and so Nana urged me to whisper these words repeatedly through the day, counting each completed phrase on a rosary, or my fingers, as I did. Those words, she said, would protect me just as they had this child in the story who would grow up to become a friend of God. *Relax, Addy, and always trust God; your life is in good hands.*

Nana's stories always made me feel better. Nana said that God tests good souls harder than others and tough challenges were blessings in disguise. So perhaps it was okay to be suffering the hurt of Dad's death. Perhaps my suffering was even a sign that I was blessed, because it made perfect sense when you heard the stories of the Chosen Ones. How much the good suffer, I thought. My Western secular outlook had made me a victim, suffering the desertion and death of my father. My Eastern outlook painted me as someone special. Someone blessed with greater trials, someone worthy of such trials. How much comfort I gained from that way of seeing things. The victor, not the victim. I would throw my shoulders back, raise my chin and be the heroine that I clearly was.

Of course, I had seen Nana read the Holy Book many times and normally I would sit quietly, waiting for her to finish, but one day soon after Dad's death, I made a shocking discovery about Nana. As she straightened the swaddling to ready the book for the high shelf where it lived, I moved next to her, opened the Holy Book randomly and pointed to a sentence in Arabic. 'Nana, what does that say?' I asked.

She pulled her lips between her teeth and looked away.

'That bit there, Nana, what does it mean?' I said, pointing again to the line of Arabic text.

She didn't answer. After a beat, or perhaps two, I understood.

Nana was a hafiz, a memoriser. She'd memorised every word of the Holy Book and other stories she'd been told. The holding of a book was a symbolic gesture, an act of reverence for the written word. Those loops and cups and peaks that danced across the page were as incomprehensible to her as they were to me. For Nana couldn't read. Not English, not Urdu, not Arabic.

It was from that day that I started writing down Nana's recipes, and alongside them, my daily musings.

It was as if the act of writing captured a part of Nana herself for ever within my words and preserved a part of my heritage which might otherwise be lost. It was this artistic endeavour which morphed eventually into my most treasured possession of all, my recipe book, a collaborative effort between me and Nana. The full working title, written in a trembling italic calligraphy I'd learned to craft at an after-school club some years back, was the snappy *MS MAYFORD'S RECIPES TO CHANGE YOUR LIFE: A MANUAL OF ART AND SCIENCE TO CHANGE HEARTS AND MINDS WITH DELICIOUS DISHES; YOUR MENTAL HEALTH COMPANION AND DAY BOOK OF ARTFUL ENDEAVOURS.* It still bears this overly long working title now, despite the years I've been writing it.

My recipe book has since been a constant work in progress: my joy and – this is not hyperbole – my *ikigai*, which is a Japanese word for the reason you get out of bed each morning.

Here are some things I learned about the art of cookery from Nana, all duly noted at page 4 of *MS MAYFORD'S RECIPES TO CHANGE YOUR LIFE.*

# Five Pillars of Artful Success in Creating Life-Changing Dishes

1. To succeed in creating a life-changing dish, it is imperative that you dissociate any emotional connection to any ingredient. For example, you may have a loathing for garlic due to an unfortunate early childhood experience, or harbour a fear of chilli. If this is the case, my sympathies are with you, but there is something crucial you must now do. You must banish any such prejudice against such food items because for success in creating life-changing dishes it is important to remove all bias.

2. Avoid short cuts. You may decide to use bottled lemon. This is a near fatal mistake because if you are lazy about such things, your dish will be lazy about delivering your wish. Think about your purpose. The changing of lives is important work.

3. Don't take advice when cooking in company. It could spell disaster and is to be avoided at all costs. Art is about what is within, not without. Cooking in company will have you wanting to please others rather than looking within to your own creative centre. The dialogue with your food is a personal exchange, and a friendly suggestion to add pepper may cut off your connection with the dish-in-formation. In fact, cooking alone is best if at all possible.

4. When you have some rare or expensive ingredient, you may feel tempted to keep it for a special occasion. Don't.

It is imperative you use it nearly straight away. How many truffle oils, walnuts in forest honey or Peruvian spice mixes, purchased with veneration, now lie abandoned on those unreachable shelves of kitchens the world over?

5. Do not be tempted to clean the kitchen while cooking. Or sort out the cutlery drawer, organise the fridge, check the post. This is mortally dangerous to the creative process. Nothing but your cookery deserves the status 'must be done', because focus is essential for the formation of your culinary masterpiece.

Understand the power of heat to transform, to reverse the forces of entropy and create order from disorder. And understand that what you create is to be imbibed into the tissues of another, into their very DNA. I believe this transformational art is alchemy and we Life-Changing Cooks are modern-day practitioners of this ancient art of transformation. Only we don't turn lead into gold but transform base ingredients into life-changing meals that can influence and heal.

A few months after Dad died an idea came to me.

I snuck out a picture of him, one I'd found hidden deep in Nana's bedside cabinet, and spoke.

'Hello, Dad,' I said. 'How are you? Aside from being . . . you know . . . dead. I just wanted to speak to you for a bit.' I straightened the picture. It was so old, all black and white and grainy. Its edges were curled and the image cracked where it had been folded. He stood with others, unknown to me. Relatives from Lahore, I guessed. 'I miss you so much, Dad. And it's okay . . . that you left. I know you loved me. I know it.' I ran my finger along a fold scarring a strike of white through his head.

I felt it then.

There was no voice, no words. Just a sense that he'd heard me. That he could see me even though I couldn't see him. Was it the memory of his love? I don't know. I held the photograph to my heart and whispered words I'd never voiced to Dad when he was around.

*I love you, Dad*, I said. *I really do.*

And it felt wonderful.

I don't remember too much about Dad because I was so young when he left. But I do remember he was like this big, overgrown kid. He'd often play with me, both of us together messing around with some toy. I always got the sense he was more interested in my toys than me. Like the time I was making a great single-brick stack of Lego, seeing how high I could go before it fell down, leaning first like some great arching stem.

'No, Addy, stay back,' he said when I tried to add another block.

'But I want to add more. I'm sure it will hold.'

'No, Addy. You sit there, stay back. Let me do it,' he said, sweeping up the sleeves of his kameez, which floated over his baggy shalwar. And so I did. He became focused, insisting I be still as he gently pressed on more and more blocks. I was certain he was holding his breath. And when they all came tumbling down, he crouched, fists clenched as if some big international sports match had been lost. I knew how much Dad loved me, so it was always strange to think of him abandoning me the way he did. His face is a blur, but I have a clear recollection of his nose. It was a great bulbous thing, the texture of satsuma skin, that looked as if it'd gone to seed. And he had this one-sided smile which made me wonder if he was only ever half-happy. He often smoothed the hair at the back of his head, which struck me as strange as he didn't have any there. Not that I recall, at least.

It embarrasses me to confess that before Gabe proposed, and despite our love, I'd never told him about my mixed heritage, in part, admittedly, because he'd never asked. He assumed I was just a Londoner, darker than most and a bit mysterious, but a Londoner nevertheless. I blame the objectifiers. When some people come to know of my heritage, I become, as if by magic, an amalgamation of the few distinct parts representing their idea of a 'Muslim'. Not a human blended of manifold elements, but a four-block Lego structure. Red: arranged marriage (*Really, I don't know how you do that!*); blue: honour killing and oppression (*I saw the Malala documentary, y'know.*

*So sad all the men from your culture want to kill you.*); green: chastity (*So you don't do* it *before marriage, eh! Really?*); yellow: headscarves (*Shouldn't you be wearing one?/How come you've got to cover your head?*). If the world's myopic eyes could only see me in this way, then I would blind them. I wasn't going to let myself be boxed and categorised because all the labels were wrong and no amount of displaying my subtle, varied self would convince them I was so much more than this combination they wanted to thrust upon me. The truth was I was no different from them. But they never got it. So, I hid my Asian roots. This was easily done, given I had looks which confused and a Western name, although people did frequently cut me a second glance, detecting something different.

And so, since Gabe never asked, I never said.

After he proposed, as we walked home under the stars, the ladle-shaped asterism of Ursa Minor above us, I finally told him that I was *both*. Both Asian and Irish. Both Muslim and Catholic. The boundaries blurred and indistinct. And was that okay with him?

Of course, needless to say, it was.

I hadn't told Nana and Mum about Gabe before the proposal. I'd only been seeing him for six months and it would have been too complicated, and besides, there was nothing to tell, until now. Ours was a household brimming with faith, so introducing Gabe to Nana and Mum was admittedly bound to have its challenges. It was a grey Friday in November and darkness was growing when we arrived at the house.

'Mum, Nana,' I said, standing in the kitchen doorway, 'this is Gabriel.'

There was no movement or acknowledgement from either of them. Just the flash of eyes as they looked between us like kittens following something sparkly.

Gabe pressed his palms together and said, 'Namaste.'

I elbowed him lightly. 'That's Hindu,' I whispered.

Furrows formed, eyebrows rose, but still the stares.

'This is Gabriel?' Nana repeated, clearly questioning.

'Yes, Nana, he's . . . he's . . .'

'The meters are under the stairs,' Mum said.

'*Nay*, no,' I said, Urdu followed by English. 'He wants to marry me.'

Nana: silence.

Mum: silence.

Gabe: silence mixed with creeping fear in his eyes.

'The gas man wants to marry you?'

'No, Nana! He's not the gas man. He's with me. He's . . .'

Mum: sharp intake of breath.

'*Shadee?* Marry? Is he Muslim?' Nana said.

Mum hard-stared her, head shaking.

'Atheist, actually,' Gabe said.

Mum: sharper intake of breath

34

'Racist!'

'No, Nana.' I said. 'He said atheist, which means he doesn't believe in God.' I felt the foolishness of my words even as I spoke them. 'But he's got a PhD,' I finished lamely.

'*Ay ya! Astagfirullah!*' Nana sang. 'A *kufar*!'

Mum took a seat.

'Well,' Gabe said with a touch of authority, 'I suppose you could say I'm more agnostic or . . . exploring. Presently at least. I'm a post-doctoral research fellow at LSE. Astrophysics and cosmology.'

A wise move, I thought. Let them know he is an educated man.

'So you've *explored* the Bible. The Quran? *Eat Pray Love*?' Mum sneered.

'But . . . well . . .' Gabe sputtered. I smelled deodorant, a rising dark odour of sweat layered beneath.

'PhD, tsk, *jahil*,' Nana hissed, which loosely translates as *ignoramus*.

Me: sharp intake of breath.

'We have to go. Nana, Mum, I'll speak to you later.' I pulled at Gabe.

'Goodbye and . . . God bless,' Gabe said, his arm rising to cross his chest just as I pulled him away.

Eventually, as is the way with those who really love you, Nana and Mum came around. They even came to like

35

Gabe, Mum treating him like a curious pet, Nana feeding him great treats and feasts when he visited. And he liked them, most of the time at least, and especially when they weren't proselytising all over him. Needless to say, Nana's Happy-Making Muffins featured regularly on the menu.

Gabe and I had a church wedding, followed within days by a Muslim nikah ceremony, so I found myself exchanging a white dress for red and gold brocade, *nude ambition* gloss for *scarlet pout* lipstick, Maybelline's sun-kissed foundation for L'Oréal's shy ivory, a feather-light wrist chain for a kilo of gold hanging from anywhere it could be attached. This dual existence was not unfamiliar to me though. It had always been this way.

Other than Nana and Mum, the only person I didn't have to explain my dual self to was my best friend Jen. Jen and I had met at school, although it was as if we'd always known each other. I recall when I first saw her blonde pigtails, pale-blue eyes and the snowy skin over her bare, lanky legs. She seemed to glow. We were in different classes, Jen in stream three and me in stream one, but that never stopped us playing together. We'd swoop like aeroplanes, arms outstretched over the school playing fields, or chase each other about on the playground in some other childish game. But we weren't best friends right away. That happened because of Elsie Ogden.

# 3

# Unpleasantness-Cancelling Lentils
(*page 14*)

To cancel unpleasantness so that lingering hurt vanishes away, take:

2 cups black urid lentils
200g butter, or a full block if you prefer
240g can kidney beans
4 tomatoes, or otherwise a 400g can will do
4 garlic cloves
thumb-sized piece of ginger
1 tsp red chilli powder
1 tsp garam masala, the king of spices
1 bay leaf

The *taste*: deep and dark and rich and buttery, with sweet undertones,
The *artistry*: showcases the heights of taste that a simple lentil can reach.
The *purpose*: to undo unpleasant feelings by smoothing them away with a creamy texture and rich flavour.

IT WAS AN UNUSUALLY HOT SPRING DAY AND JEN AND I were making piles out of the faded grass cuttings the mower hadn't managed to collect, competing to see who could make the largest pile. After a while we gave up and lay back on the cool, freshly cut grass, surrounded by the scent of summer. I cast my eyes up and fell into the endless blue expanse. Just then, Elsie Ogden, a burly fifth former, shouted something abusive I didn't understand.

'Oi, you. D'you hear what I said?' she taunted.

I had heard her words but hadn't appreciated in that moment that they were targeted at me. Elsie's name-calling and bully tactics were a regular occurrence, but it never went beyond an elbowing in the corridor or being hissed at in class. It was common knowledge that she had a difficult home life, but there was something more today. Something edgy and urgent in her manner.

'You heard me . . . s'why don't you just go home, you . . .'

At this, the whole playground fell silent. People edged forward as a single mass towards us. There is something deeply embarrassing about being the target of an insult. Particularly before others and especially when you don't know what it means. I felt my heart rate rise and my stomach fall. Why was she insisting I go home to Spitalfields when it was only lunchtime? And what was that word she had called me? I had the misplaced urge, being academically minded, to immediately go and look it up, until a small cluster of hungry-eyed onlookers started searching about to see who Elsie was after. I remember wondering if I too should pretend I was searching about, in the hope of fooling everyone that I was not the target. But Elsie approached me, fists clenched, scowl on her face, her great square width and pulpy skin eclipsing the gathered bodies about. Both Jen and I stood. Elsie, now facing me in a stand-off, leaned forward and scowled. I leaned forward too, arms straight down at my sides, fists balled. I, of course, was just mirroring; Elsie could crush me with her left thigh.

'You hear me . . . get lost . . .'

That word again. I could think of nothing to say in response.

And then something happened that I could never have

predicted. Jen moved forward and stood, legs astride, arms folded, between Elsie and me, forming a barrier, her petite frame a 'David' before the 'Goliath' of Elsie's. Next, and without the slightest evidence of fear, she said in thin single words, 'Leave. Her. Alone.'

There was a pause. Nobody knew what would happen next. And then Elsie grabbed one of Jen's pigtails and yanked it so hard that she tumbled to the ground. In a flash of blinding fury, every part of me tense, teeth clenched, a force of instinct overtook me and I charged at Elsie. Before I knew it, I had bull-rammed her and we fell in a seemingly endless tumble down a grass verge. I stood up panting, adrenaline blazing, blood thumping. When Elsie got to her feet, her sidekicks materialising like djinn, Jen was again beside me, cute as a Barbie doll despite her bared teeth and hands balanced on hips: my very own Wonder Woman.

The gathered crowd started chanting, 'Fight, fight, fight,' in time with the thudding of blood in my ears.

My heartbeat said, *Youcan, youcan, youcan,* seemingly in defiance of the words in my head, which were, *Help! Help! Help!*

Then Elsie charged and I ducked, head-butting her in the chub of her gut. Next came a shard of light, followed by dark. When focus returned, Elsie and I were both lying side by side on our backs, staring skywards as if enjoying the charms of the summer day. We scrambled back to our feet and she stepped forward again. The crowd fell silent, their blood-lust palpable.

We must have stood there like that for what seemed like for ever. And then Elsie grunted like an animal, tossed her chin, turned and walked away, her sidekicks in tow. Just like that. No hiss of abuse, no face-making, no posturing to resume the fight.

As she did, my courage mounted enough for me to call out behind her, 'And I won't go home . . . it's only lunch time!' I realised immediately how lame a retort that was and nearly wet myself with fear that she might turn back. But she didn't.

We might have won the fight, but truth be told, Elsie Ogden's words hurt me like a burn to the skin. That someone sees you as different is one thing, but to go so far as to publicly show their hatefulness was another. When I came to know the meaning of the abuse, that I was less in her eyes because of my foreign blood, I took to hiding parts of myself. Parts of who I was, my foreignness, my heritage. In short, everything that made me different, my singular aim being to mix in with the majority, all in the name of blending in so I could be 'normal' like everyone else.

The only good thing about that day was that Jen and I became best friends. It was like she could see who I really was. Not as an amalgam of four Lego blocks, but me as a whole with all my subtleties. Around her, I could relax, be myself. Of course, we had our differences, but we always made up in the end. We were like sisters in that way.

On the day of that first altercation with Elsie Ogden, I returned from school with a sad face and grazed knees. When Mum asked me how it'd happened, I said I'd tripped. And then, to stop the onslaught of further questions, I asked her, as she dabbed Germolene on my knee, what she could tell me about Pakistan.

'Why do you want to know, Addy? Is it because of . . .' she said in her sing-song Irish lilt as she examined my knee. She didn't finish her question, but I knew she was asking if it was because of Dad because, as always when Dad was mentioned, she pressed her lips tight and turned a subtle shade of pink. Mum was given to rapid colour change with her pale Irish skin, moving in moments on a spectrum ranging from rose pink to blotchy magenta. She took a deep breath and then said no more.

Not with words, at least.

Because there was that familiar look in her eyes as she observed me. When she gave me The Squint, I knew she didn't see me, but the part of me formed by Dad. When Dad left, he didn't go empty-handed. He took with him Mum's smile and that kernel of softness within her I had known before he went. What remained was mostly a brittle outer shell. Mum threw herself into her work, retreating into silence as if she was trying to rub herself out. She hardly spoke, but when she did, she transformed into an irascible and unforgiving person, habitually sharp-tongued, supporting all manner of grudges in varying degrees and intensities. She had a bone to pick with everybody. There'd been a few thirty-second tantrums I'd paid for with what felt to me to be a year of hard looks. This personality shift began to show on her face, giving her a pinched look which was only intensified by her thin tight lips. And so, despite her fluffy bobbed hair, she cut a surprisingly stern figure.

Mum imposed a ban on any photographs in which Dad featured. Nana and I both had to keep ours hidden away, for fear they'd be destroyed. I think that was why I cherished my photo of him so much, the one I would at times speak to. There was also an unvoiced ban on speaking Dad's name and, if he must be mentioned, he was referred to simply as 'him' (generally voiced with a snarl), 'the ghost', 'the vanishing man', or most often, 'that shite'. Dad leaving confirmed the curse of the Mayford household. It had happened to her mother before and her grandmother before that. The men didn't stay. So abandonment, for Mum, was the ultimate sin. *You can do anything, say anything, but you don't leave your own*, she would say. This I've absorbed into my own moral fabric.

Mum always stressed that Dad's leaving us had nothing, absolutely nothing to do with me, which served only to settle firmly within me the idea that it was entirely my fault. And I couldn't help thinking that if he hadn't left, perhaps he would still be alive.

After cleaning my knee and replacing the cap on the Germolene, Mum walked over to the framed tapestry of the Serenity Prayer on the kitchen door. She always did this when she was frustrated or upset. She crossed her arms, pulling in deep breaths as she did. I followed her, crossed my arms like Mum and stared at it too. God grant me, the prayer said, [deep breath] the serenity to accept the things I cannot change, [deep breath] the courage to [deep breath] change the things I can [deep breath], and the wisdom to know the difference . . .

She returned to her chores as Nana walked in. 'Addy fell,' she told Nana with a raised eyebrow. They exchanged quiet words, Nana handing Mum a cup of tea as they glanced over at me in turn. It was always like this. Mum and Nana were like comrades, chatting over the weather, the news, planning things needing to be done at home and laughing together at some joke I didn't understand. It was only when it came to dealing with me that a certain formality arose between them.

With Nana it was different. I hadn't told Mum about Elsie Ogden, but as soon as she was out of earshot, I told Nana the truth. All the details of what had happened at school. Nana did what she always did when I was upset, and made me Unpleasantness-Cancelling Lentils. She placed black lentils called urid onto the hob to boil with a tin of kidney beans and then separately fried tomatoes in a whole block of butter, scattering a special spice mix upon it in readiness for step two. These were the ingredients of her luscious, creamy Unpleasantness-Cancelling Lentils, otherwise known as Butter Daal or Daal Makhani. As she cooked, she would silently mouth a prayer, which she would cast into the room by exhaling as if the power of the words lay caught in the hollow of her mouth and must be carried by breath into the room. Sometimes she'd blow the prayer she'd mouthed right onto me. One of my most abiding memories is her soft breath, cool upon my face.

'Let's cancel the unpleasantness, shall we?' she'd say.

The dish healed, lifted and supported me whenever the need arose, and the healing would be so complete that afterwards I could hardly remember what it was that had ailed me just moments earlier. I would float in a bliss-filled bubble of sensation, tastes, scents, textures, so lost in the experience that all else would shrink into oblivion, at least for a while. It was a wonder what these recipes could do.

In the years to come, I think Nana knew whenever I'd had an Elsie Ogden day, even the times I didn't tell her, because she'd place a little extra turmeric in the meal and trickle manuka honey into my mouth before bed. Sometimes she'd take a pinch of black onion seeds, those inky black commas with mystical healing properties, and get me to swallow them with a glass of water.

Nana always dried my tears, even as she cried her own, weeping for those who'd walked away: her father, her husband, her son. I'll not lie. Nana was tough, often overbearing. If there was a way to do it, it had to be hers. But I loved her. Because every part of me was formed in the curved cradle of her body. She had flown across oceans, leaving her whole family behind. Endured cold British weather in saris. And she did this all for me. To build me a shelter of her own blood and bones. *I will never disown you*, she said, as if in answer to the shadowy ghost of Dad's absence.

Yes, I loved Nana.

Later that night after my first altercation with Elsie Ogden, I took the picture of Dad out from between the leaves of my Ms Mayford recipe book and placed it before me on my bedside table. I had wanted to tell him about the bullies, but instead, as I touched the image, a memory came to me of the time Dad had taken me to the local park. The swing was much too small for him, but he still sat on it and swung alongside me. When we got tired, we straddled the swings and Dad spoke to me about Pakistan.

'Addy, one day I will take you to Lahore. It is beautiful but much too hot. I will take you to a *mithai* sweet shop.'

'Do they make chocolate?'

'No, *beta*. They hand-make the most delicious sweets on the street in front of you in big vats of oil. So many, like *ladoo*, *patisa*, *gulab jamun*, *jalebi*, *barfi* . . .' The list went on a while.

'What are they like, Daddy?'

'How can I describe? Each is so different. *Patisa* is crystallised vegetable that becomes crispy and oozes rose-scented syrup when you bite it. *Barfi* tastes like vanilla and ice-cream, only much richer. And my favourite is something called a *besan ke ladoo*, made out of gram flour. It is dry and crumbly and crispy at the same time. Savoury and sweet and nutty.' Dad licked his lips.

'I can't wait, Daddy. What's Lahore like?'

'Lahore? Lahore is alive. Everyone is so busy, and you can buy anything there. Like real fresh milk on the street because a man will be milking his cow in front of you. And gold, clothes, food at very big marketplaces like the market of Anarkali. Did you know Anarkali means pomegranate but it's also the name of a beautiful young lady who was murdered? The market is named after her because she's buried at a tomb near Anarkali Bazaar.' Dad stared at the middle distance, lost in thought. He looked sad. I think he missed Lahore. I tried to work out what made Mum and Dad argue so much, but I never could. They seemed perfectly happy until they were in the same room.

'Was she a princess?'

'No, but she was killed because this prince fell in love with her. The prince's father became very angry, so he chased her out of the city and then had her buried alive.'

This sounded gruesome and a lot like the stories of the Arabian Nights that Nana would tell me. A king murdering a virgin bride each day, and Scheherazade bravely saving young girls from this murderous king by spinning her yarns.

'Do kings always kill women then?' I said.

Dad looked puzzled.

'It's just that Nana tells a story of a king who kills women too.'

'No, *beta*. They're just stories.'

I was not convinced.

'I will take you to Anarkali Bazaar some day and we can visit Anarkali's tomb.' He smiled as he flattened the invisible hair at the back of his neck.

Most of my memories of childhood, of grey days, school, walking the streets of London with Nana and Mum, are cast in black and white. But there is one rainbow-coloured exception. When I was six, around the time Dad left, Nana took me to Pakistan. I didn't realise it at the time, but she must have been following him out there. It was the only time I've ever been. I recall being lifted out of the windows of a train and handed through the air from person to person, each clasping me in an urgent embrace before handing me on. My cheeks kissed, pulled, lovingly slapped. *Guria*, dolly, a real live dolly. Addy, baby. And the flowers. The scent of damp and sweet in the air: *chameli*, the jasmine flower, marigold, the flower of Mary, roses all bound into patterned bracelets and slipped on my arms until no more could fit. Strangers claiming kin swinging me about in an endlessly rotating embrace; garlands appearing about my neck, dense and full of the weight of their affections.

I remember a train journey that went on for days and nights, mini-market stalls forming at our carriage window at every stop, old ladies in jaunty colourful prints selling thick sweet chai made from the milk of buffalo, young grime-covered boys in muted dirt-coloured clothing offering trays of sparkling bangles and juddering bead earrings calling, 'Bargain! Bargain!' The air thick with unfamiliar scents. I was afraid, like a kitten, hiding in Nana's sari, seeing the world through its green and yellow folds. We arrived somewhere in the dark of night, and I wondered how I'd acquired a new name: *guria*, dolly. Later, I would discover everyone had love-names. Real names were for passports and college entrances. Love-names, names filled with familiarity and affection, were given by family to mark you as theirs. To tell the world you belonged.

These memories form an endless stream of sights and sounds and scents, unbroken by the normal passage of night and day or time and place. I am in the marketplace, engulfed in multi-coloured powders or staring at sacks of the mangled remains of what used to be fruit or leaves; spice stalls a riot of scent and colour, and fabric being pressed against shoulder and knee; vibrant colours and prints, which as if by magic are morphed the next day into dresses with trousers that match. Everywhere I go, people touch my hair, comment on my pale skin, pinch my cheeks. Nana shuffles me about introducing me to endless, faceless people, toying with me as if I'm a doll on a shelf; stroking my hair, tapping my nose, tickling me. When the world falls quiet, alone in our room, I see Nana go sad. Dad isn't around any more. I want to ask why, but I'm afraid to. Nana prays, forehead to the ground. I wonder if it is God who is making her sad, because when she rises just before dawn for *namaz*, the morning prayers, on her prayer mat, she cries. I remember the distant hiss and hum of each day as it starts, the scent of warm earth mingled with the coriander-fresh night air seeping through insect screens. She prays for him, for Dad to come back. Always Dad, I am sure. She looks over at me, over and over, as she prays and gets sadder, the prayers always ending in tears.

Dad reappears just as we are returning to the UK. I am so happy. I hold his hand and won't let go. Then, at the airport, he leaves. He's not coming on the plane with us. I'm crying and screaming, but he won't come.

We're back in London and he's not. *Back to Lahore*, are the words I hear whispered in the corner of rooms, eyes sliding over to me and away. *Distract her, she won't notice, she's still a child*. But of course I notice. I ask them over and over. *Where is Dad? Why has he gone away?* And then over time I avoid the questions that make them look away.

# 4

# Lose Your Rage Chicken Korma
## (*page 17*)

For rage to be doused, so that composure can return, take:

6-8 chicken pieces, boned or boneless
1 onion, sliced
6 cloves garlic, chopped
½ tbsp butter, melted and warm
½ tsp red chilli powder
½ tsp cumin powder
plenty of yogurt, say 4 tbsp
2 tbsp coriander seed powder (the secret of the taste)

The taste: simple comfort, mind-blowing flavour, like affection
in a warm and meaty gravy.
The artistry: the power of one particular spice (ground
coriander seeds) to singularly transform.
The purpose: to instil deep calm and peace so the fires of
rage die down; be warned, unlikely friendships may also form.

I'M NOT GOING TO SAY GROWING UP WAS EASY. ELSIE AND her gang remained a fixture for the next few years. Sometimes I surrendered to their abuse, returning home pinched and scratched from the hits and kicks, from Elsie coming at me clenched and red with vengeance, her sidekicks at her shoulders, rhythms thumping in my ears, my feet, my chest.

Sometimes I managed a thump in return before running or succumbing. But it carried on and on, becoming a familiar pattern, rotating with the inevitable predictability of night and day. The spite, the hate, the anger. But I never broke. I was tough. As tough as Elsie Ogden and her goons, at least.

Nana's recipes helped. Whenever I returned home tight with rage, Nana would feed me Lose Your Rage Chicken Korma, a creamy dish with a yogurt base that never failed to loosen my fury. Nana would whisper as she tucked me into bed. 'Addy,' she would say, 'nothing that hits you was ever going to miss you. And nothing that misses you was ever going to hit you. Rest easy, my child. You're in good hands. God's hands. Have patience, because patience is prayer. Your only job: choose. Choose the right thing to do in any situation. Whatever happens is a blessing or a lesson. Always.'

She was right.

Just a few years later, when school finished, two great things happened. First, I got a job as a chef. And second, I met Gabe.

# 5

# Come Together Spice Mix (Garam Masala) (*page 20*)

For differing elements to combine and lead you to places and people you could never otherwise find, take:

cloves
black peppercorns
cumin seeds
coriander seeds
black cardamom pods
cinnamon
(to be combined in secret proportions by expert hands)

The taste: perfumed and rich, opening up another dimension of taste.
The artistry: life is a mix of different parts. Garam masala proves they cannot only live together well but can carry each other to heights each part singularly could never reach.
The purpose: to show how difference is not to be feared but embraced with open arms.

MEETING GABE, THAT DIZZY HIGH POINT OF MY LIFE, happened at a dinner party at Jen's parents' house. I'd just turned eighteen, completed my A-levels, and started a new job at a local eatery called Arabian Delights, while Jen had become a Boots make-up artist. I had secured a place at university but turned it down because the only thing I ever wanted to study was cookery. It took Mum a while to forgive me. She had seen great poverty as a child, often citing the nights her family shared two meals between her five siblings, or the nights they had no dinner at all. She wanted a grand education for me, followed by a big career, and certainly a better future than cooking for a living. For the longest time she would scowl when I entered a room. To be fair, the pay at Arabian Delights was derisory, and the place had all the hallmarks of a dead-end job. But I couldn't afford to attend a decent culinary school yet. It was just a foot in the door, a door I intended on keeping open as I worked out how to advance my cookery career. That night at Jen's place, though, I began to see a different future.

Gabe was a friend of Jen's family who we'd been told would be joining us for dinner that night. When he entered the room, Jen was teasing me about my refusal to even consider an arranged marriage.

'So,' she said, 'if your Nana finds you some gorgeous hunk, you'll be all, "No, no, leave me alone . . ."'

'I will,' I said. 'I'm not ready for a serious relationship . . .'

At exactly that moment, Gabe walked in. Seven pairs of eyes around the table jumped up to his gorgeous face. He, however, looked only at me, and as he did, everything in our circumference turned to a blur in a momentary halo of silence. I wished I could swallow back my previous words. I was, in that moment, quite ready. He had a hesitant manner, reminiscent of someone who'd realised they'd entered the wrong house.

'. . . don't you think, Addy?' Jen said.

I realised I hadn't heard a word she'd said prior to those last four. I smiled inanely in the hope that would constitute a response of sorts, then, dropping the smile, I turned swiftly back to Gabe, who had taken the seat opposite.

'Okay, I'll warn any gorgeous guy to stay away from you then,' Jen teased.

This was not the message I wanted broadcast, so I changed the subject post-haste to the food presently being served. I took a bite.

'Mmm, delicious,' I said. It was disgusting. But I was less distracted by such culinary ineptness, because he was staring at me across the table. Why had I never seen him at Jen's house before? He was tall and slender, with milk-chocolate hair and molten brown eyes. He had a wide stretch to his shoulders from which his fine jumper seemed to hang perfectly, exposing his strong forearms. He was still staring. I appreciate the word *stare* suggests a certain impertinence, but his stare was anything but. I became self-conscious, cheeks burning with the growing wish I'd put more make-up on, more stylish clothing, been born a more stylish person generally. I started fiddling with my hair, then flicked up my eyes. His were still on me. This was starting to feel unbearable in the most pleasant of ways.

'Aren't you Jen's best friend, Addy?'

*He knows me!*

'That's right,' I said, holding out my hand, which he shook with a firm grasp. His warm cinnamon scent reached me from across the table.

'I'm Gabriel.' Then, after a pause, 'This looks delicious.' He took a bite.

'It is,' I said, while scrunching my toes inside my shoes to urge myself past my nerves. 'What do you like to eat mostly, Gabriel?'

'Please, call me Gabe,' he said. 'My favourite has to be curry. I love spicy food.'

Heavens above! If this wasn't a sign . . .

We then proceeded to have a conversation about the components of an excellent garam masala spice mix.

'The cumin must go into the blender first and be powdered before the cloves touch it,' I said.

'So there are cloves in it too.'

'Oh yes. It would never work without cloves. The flavour would be lacking. The final dish would be "like a beautiful woman with only one eye".'

'That's a famous quote, isn't it?'

'That's right,' I said, 'they're the words of the one and only Brillat-Savarin.'

He smiled widely and nodded. All the while, his eyes never left mine. 'So tell me, Addy, what else goes in . . . ?'

'Well,' I said, pausing to create the appearance of intelligent thought, 'there are five basic spices.'

'Black peppercorns?'

'That's right,' I said. 'Have you made garam masala before?'

'Oh no, no. I'm guessing.' He raised his hands. Large, angular hands. Manly hands.

'Ah,' I said. 'Well, those big black cardamoms also go in. Not the little green ones. The black ones smell like a combination of earth, wood and spice. Most people don't know about them.' He looked genuinely engaged. 'But see, the real secret is the proportions with which the spices are combined.'

'Interesting.'

'Why don't you come and sample one of my meals first-hand, where I work, at Arabian Delights? I use garam masala all the time.' My breathing was now un-even, between the myriad thuds and beats in my ears and chest. Onlookers would observe a prosaic exposition of the constituents of that king of all spice mixes, but there was no doubt to me that this was a blazing courtship. Before he could answer, there was a tittering of laughter to my left. Jen had placed her red scarf upon her head and was posing.

'You look like Little Red Headscarf with that on your head.'

'You mean Little Red Riding Hood,' said Jen's mother.

'No, I don't. Don't you know the story?' I said. 'Nana's told it to me so many times.'

'We've all heard it, Addy, and it's a hood, not a headscarf.'

'Perhaps yours is a different story. This is the story of a young girl who was asked to take some *ladoo* sweets to her grandmother, who lived in the woods.'

'That's hysterical, Ads,' Jen said. 'That's what happens in "Little Red Riding Hood".'

'So does the Hoodie girl also meet a djinn?' The table fell silent.

'Listen,' I said, speaking the words with emphasis, 'she was called Little Red Headscarf because she loved to wear a red headscarf, even though there were many other colour choices available to her. Her mother was concerned as the sun was lower in the sky than she would have liked. "Do not stray off the beaten track because the spirit people come out at dusk." Little Red Headscarf promised she wouldn't. As it happened, she did move off the track, to pick some flowers, and that's where she met a wolf, who asked her where she was going.'

Someone I couldn't identify snorted, stifling a laugh.

'Are you teasing?' Gabe said. 'That's the Riding Hood story.' I gave him a stern look, which prompted him to smile and raise his hands in defence. I wished he would keep them there, in full view.

'Just listen. Because this was not in fact a wolf, but a djinn.' I said the word djinn with danger, extending it on my tongue. 'You probably don't know what they are. Djinn are those shape-shifting beings also created with free will, like us human beings. When the djinn found out where Little Red Headscarf was going, he rushed to her grandmother's home and entered her through her mouth, possessing her completely. After Little Red

Headscarf arrived at her grandmother's house, she could tell something was wrong. Her grandmother was ill in bed.

'*What big eyes you have, Grandma,*' she said.

'*All the better to see you with.*'

'*What big ears you have, Grandma.*'

'*All the better to hear you with.*'

'*What a big mouth you have,*' she said.

'*All the better to eat you with.*'

'And Little Red Headscarf was about to be taken by the djinn when she ran screaming into the woods. A huntsman heard her screams and only managed to spot her because of her bright red headscarf bobbing up and down in a clearing. When the huntsman reached the djinn, he said the magic prayer, *I seek refuge in God from Satan, the accursed one,* because the devil is from the race of djinn. With that, the djinn shape-shifted to his original form and flew away. Most likely it was an ifrit; Nana says they're the mightiest kind of djinn. The grandmother and Little Red Headscarf were saved. The end.'

There was a little flutter of applause.

'Amazing story, Addy. Do you have more?' Gabe said. I blushed, nodding.

'That djinn in Nana's story, Addy. It's meant to be a wolf,' Jen said. 'It eats the grandmother and they save her by cutting her out of its stomach.'

'But Jen, that makes no sense,' I said, 'don't you see?

65

There'd be all this blood and guts. The grandmother would undoubtedly have sustained mortal injuries. And a wolf cannot speak or morph into a convincing human form. No. It's definitely a djinn possession. And shape-shifting and mischief are the hallmarks of djinn-folk, who've been known for centuries to play such tricks.'

Jen was dumbfounded. I noticed Gabe watching me, the slightest smile on his lips and eyes. He took a deep breath, released it slowly. I cannot say, but I think he was having the same difficulty steadying his breathing as me.

# 6

# Love Me Forever Lamb (*page 23*)

For feelings of love and adoration to arise, lifting desire to untold heights, take:

8-10 chunks of lamb, boned or boneless
1 onion, sliced, to be fried
garam masala, the king of spice mixes, whole, not ground (1 tsp peppercorn, 5 cloves, 1 tsp cumin seeds, 5cm/2in cinnamon stick, 2 large black cardamom pods)
4 tbsp yogurt (100-150g)
2.5cm/1in ginger
6 cloves garlic, minced
3 tomatoes, chopped
handful fresh coriander, chopped
salt to taste
boiled basmati rice, as desired

The *taste*: spicy and meaty with underlying sweet notes.
The *artistry*: the melding of basic ingredients to transform the simple to the sophisticated.
The *purpose*: to connect souls with deep intimacy and unlock desires.

THE NEXT DAY, AT WORK AT ARABIAN DELIGHTS, I couldn't stop thinking about Gabe. Thinking, though, implies my mind casually ambling over to a memory and observing it. This, in contrast, was a full-on, high-definition replay, with additional imaginings that never actually happened, imaginings that I could not repeat here without blushing. I wallowed in these fantasies, played them over and over, edited, added to, varied then replayed. The problem was we'd never arranged to meet. We hadn't even exchanged contact details.

'Addy,' Omar said when he saw me staring blindly at nothing, 'come help me.' Omar Al Khalili was the proprietor of Arabian Delights, and a great balloon of a man. Every part of him was wide and round: his face, his nose, his torso and even his forearms and back. He had a heavy accent and two operational speeds, slow and desperately slow, and this shuffle which had me wondering if his hips were fused to his femur. It gave him an air of confidence, even though he took too long to get anywhere. Omar was always in his shop, always wearing the same perplexed expression. The world wasn't designed for him. It was as if he'd been beamed here from some desert oasis between sips of *Kahwar* tea and dates. Omar could manage working with bare flames and a knife, but any other device was for him a conundrum. I'd regularly find him challenged by the food processor, or suspiciously eyeing up the knobs on his oven.

'I have two orders from the machine,' he said. As he was currently staring at the computer, I understood he was referring to the 'machine' from which Just Eat orders would arrive as if by magic, an event Omar was still dubious about.

Arabian Delights was a small, canteen-style shop. The fish tank in the window was a little like those you sometimes find in the fronts of Chinese restaurants. Inside, the place housed four wooden benches set with white garden chairs which were rarely ever occupied. I walked around avoiding the cracks in the floor tiles with every step I took, a throwback to a distant memory of a game I would play as a child with Dad.

'It's a complaint, Omar. See?' I said pointing at the screen. 'They weren't happy with the meal.'

'Offer them a free meal on us, Addy – write it on

the machine,' Omar said, jabbing his finger at the computer.

'What's the point of always doing that? How are you going to make any money that way?'

'Money,' Omar said. 'Money comes from God, not from' – he leaned into the computer – 'James Redbridge. Trust in God . . .'

'. . . but tie up your camel,' I completed. This was Omar's favourite saying and I always finished it, though Omar was all trust and no tying. Preparing a free meal to placate customer disappointment was his most frequently used policy, one that had spread about and was most likely being abused. Everyone knew Arabian Delights would never amount to anything much.

'It's for takeaway, Addy,' Omar said, handing me ingredients as he heaved his swaddled gut to the left. The onion and garlic were ready to be part of a meal. I could tell as they had started peeling themselves. I moved the crispy curls of onion and flakes of garlic skin aside.

Several times a week I would enter into intense discussions with Omar on techniques, new recipes, unusual vegetables. Being around anyone in the throes of creating a meal – the scents, the sounds, the endless possibilities presented by the morphing, melting, combining and coalescing of ingredients – was my idea of perfect sanctuary. I only wished there was more of it going on at

Arabian Delights, or that I could be at some busy, famous fusion restaurant, cooking for many people and honing my skills. At times, I was disappointed to see Omar's lack of enthusiasm for The Art.

My time at Arabian Delights included assisting Omar in preparatory work such as chopping onions, cleaning pans, preparing salad and boiling rice. Ancillary support tasks. Sometimes he'd let me do more, even allowing me to prepare an entire order by myself. At those times, I felt like a virtuoso performer rather than a supporting member of an orchestra. I particularly vied for the opportunity to cook on those occasions a customer actually entered the shop, as opposed to for takeout orders. I would reason to Omar that I should be allowed to cook for the walk-ins, to ensure high standards of 'customer service'; Omar was slower than me, I would say, and it was imperative we didn't keep walk-in customers waiting too long in such a bleak environment (although I'd refrain from voicing the 'bleak environment' bit).

When I was done with the onions and garlic, my thoughts returned to Gabe and whether I'd see him again. I wandered over to the fish tank in the window and started fantasising. The hawkfish was perched on a stone throne, presiding over little flat fish scudding first to the left then to the right, and the regal tang was busy poking about the rocks. I was distracted by a blur on the other side of the tank. A customer? I stood. Outside on the street, looking up at the sign, his face glowing green in the fluorescent light, was Gabe.

I pull at the door, my heart drum-rolling. I feel faint.

'Gabriel?' I say, my intonation questioning.

'Addy.' His stare sets off a Catherine wheel inside my gut.

'You came.'

'I did.' He smiles. I can't breathe. 'How could I not?'

'I . . .' The words send my Catherine wheel spinning out of control.

An awkward pause, mercifully broken by Gabe. 'Shall I come in?'

I realise I'm blocking him. I pull the door wide. 'Sorry . . . !'

'No, no.' He looks at me. A motionless stare. His eyes incandescent, melted chocolate being stirred. 'So. I would love to try one of those dishes you were talking about. I can't tell you how good it sounded as I was eating that tasteless, white . . . was it pasta?'

'Not by my definition.'

'And perhaps you have another story? "Snow White and the Seven Sheikhs", "Aladdin and the Teapot"?'

'You're mocking me.'

'No, not at all, I love . . .' a heart-stopping pause, 'hearing your stories. Just wondering if there are more.'

I breathe in deep. 'Oh, so many. Hours of them, hours, like, like . . .' I raise my hands, words smouldering to ash again.

'Good. Perhaps one tonight, with . . . any suggestions from the menu?' He squints at the dense, illegible typescript.

'Oh, I have the perfect dish for you, something you will love. It's a lamb dish called Love . . . I mean Lamb.'

'Creative. A lamb dish called Lamb. I like it.' He nods meaningfully.

'I mean . . .' I pull in a deep breath. 'Take a seat and I'll pop back when it's done.' I run to the rear of the shop and hang on to the worktop, hands slipping on sliced onion. I cover my face with my hand, bits of onion still stuck to my palms, bringing tears to my eyes. *OhmyGod, ohmyGod*, I say. This goes on for a while, until Omar returns from the store room.

'A customer, Addy, see,' he says, pointing at Gabe.

'I know, Omar. Hands off. He's mine.' There is gravitas in my voice. Omar steps back, jaw open.

'Omar,' I say, 'trust me. You know I'm your lucky charm.'

The name I had stumbled over was a Nana special: Love Me Forever Lamb. This was my chance to use the power of my cookery to win Gabe over. Could I pull it off?

Pausing to calm my nerves, I began. First, fry the onions, then add the lamb with the whole spices, yogurt, half a tub, crushed garlic, tomatoes and a sprinkle of crushed dried chillies over the sizzling mix. I *buned* the dish to perfection (*buning* being a technique where the dish is cooked on a high heat, wok style, only it goes on a while). The whole spices danced between the squares of lamb in the rich tomato and onion-based sauce. As I started work on a side salad, I noticed Omar watching me through narrowed eyes, his chubby face pulled into his regular smile of curiosity and concentration. I'd seen it before, the same perplexed stare whenever I'd become possessed with the preparation of a meal. I poured in a little cinnamon-infused melted butter, trickled in star anise water, adjusted the garlic, pepper, mustard, salt, in exact proportions, stirring and directing the meal as it wanted me to.

Leaning over the pan, I inhaled. I detected each ingredient as distinct from each other – the yoghurt, the spice, the cumin – even as they melded in combination. It was as visible to me as the sweeps of an artist's brush. The requirements for brilliance didn't come to me as a list of steps; it was never like that. I was an artist with vision, the dish an artwork in progress. I was simply responding to those mysterious, creative urges welling up from the art-in-progress itself. I knew the hues to be applied and exactly where they were needed.

I trickled a little maple syrup, dusted salt, sprinkled coriander leaves, balanced textures, increased fire, allowed some charring, then cooled with a spill of water. I was unstoppable, possessed with the desire to create something great, something life-changing, something that could win me Gabe's heart. Finally, near completion, I sampled a jot of the sauce. Something was missing. What could it be? I went deep into that special place within where art is born, where I was oblivious of all else. Alone, but not lonely, focused but free. And it came to me in a delirious flash of light. Vinegar. Plain, unassuming table vinegar. I took it off the shelf and tricked the tart tea-coloured fluid over the dancing bubbles: three tablespoons and a dash more.

Towards the end I whispered something like a prayer, an incantation, a spell. Whatever you call it, as the meal neared completion, marked by the oil sitting visibly above the sauce, I poured my feelings and wishes over it. I felt it then. That feeling I get in the throes of creation, that glimmer of transcendence. *Lecto divino*. It lasted for the briefest moment, the feeling my life had ultimate meaning and that I was living that meaning. Finally, I topped off the meal with three twists of pink Himalayan salt, a sprinkle of coriander leaves and a dusting of chilli flakes, more for decorative effect.

It was ready.

I stepped out to Gabe and served him my Love Me

Forever Lamb, urging the meal to fulfil the purpose for which it was created. I watched him from behind a pillar as he ate.

Watched him swoon with delight.

It worked.

Seven meals and a few months later, he was mine.

And if that's not magic, I don't know what is.

After Gabe proposed, I started planning the life we would lead meticulously, just like one of my recipes. Details, methodologies, time frames. My priorities had changed, and Gabe insisted I leave Arabian Delights and put my dream of becoming a professional chef on hold so that he and I could set up home and raise a family. Omar was devastated, but I agreed because it seemed so important to Gabe. And everything fell into place. Well, almost everything.

After a year of trying and waiting and waiting and trying, I hadn't got pregnant. It didn't make sense. After all, I was young and healthy. I started to develop an anxious urgency for it to happen. Life took on a looped pattern, repeating with each lunar cycle. But no matter how patiently we waited, how persistently we tried, it didn't happen. When after a further six months we still hadn't conceived, we finally went to a fertility clinic for tests. Few things can match the creeping tension of waiting to become pregnant or the weight of disappointment when every month your body lets you down, except, perhaps, waiting for the result of tests. But, as they say, life goes on.

# THE DAY

# 7

## Amorous Chilli Chocolate
*(page 27)*

For feelings of love which rise to great passion, take:

200g chocolate, melted and smooth
3 egg yolks
4 egg whites, beaten with sugar to taste, to be folded in to
the chocolate
1 tbsp saffron-infused water
1/2 tsp red chilli, or more to taste
150ml double cream

The taste: sensual, sweet and warm.
The artistry: to draw people in by the comfort of the
familiar to a place of untold desire.
The purpose: to stir passions and arouse tender, sensuous
feelings of longing and love.

# 7.30am

The day everything changed started like any other. When I came out of the shower, Gabe was awake, propped up in bed, flicking through his phone. Unusually, I was up before him, as he had enrolled me onto a class at Le Cordon Bleu, to learn pastry-making techniques for a birthday treat. It was a place where I dreamed I would one day train.

Gabe looked happy, arms and legs akimbo, as if he'd been dropped from the ceiling onto an explosion of quilt and sheet. Being with him still felt new and exciting, even after nearly two years. Wrapped in a towel, with strands of my hair wet about my shoulders, I smiled. It was a one-sided smile, triggered by thoughts of the previous night. My mouth filled with the memory of Amorous Chilli Chocolate, the dish I had created the night before, now a regular part of my repertoire. Gabe responded with a wink, his eyes following the trails of water running down my shoulders from my drenched hair. I ignored his lifting of the sheets to invite me back in.

We'd moved into a maisonette around the corner from Nana and Mum. Whenever I walked through our home, I could smell his particular scent wherever Gabe had been: the bedroom for a bit, hovering in the hall where we had an extensive display of wedding photos. (We couldn't agree on which photo we liked the best, so all ten were set out in a zig-zag of silver frames.)

I reached into my wardrobe, the door of which was ajar with the pressure of a jumble of clothes, then gave Gabe my worried look.

'Are you sure you're okay to fix your own dinner tonight?' Cordon Bleu had invited the guests on this course to join them for dinner after the session.

'Yes, Squid.' Squid was my pet name. 'A sandwich is also food, Ads. I will survive.'

'Not sure your variety of sandwich qualifies as food.'

'Depends on how you define it.' He fiddled with his phone as I ran my fingers through my hair. 'You're such a snob, Ads. What have I done, sending you off to Gordon Bleu?'

I flashed him a fake, pouty frown. 'Jesus, Gabe! It's

*Cordon* Bleu. You're thinking of Gordon Ramsay.'

'Okay.' Speaking into his phone, he said, 'Let's see. Hey, Siri – define food.'

The electronic voice replied, *Food means any nutritious substance that animals eat in order to maintain life and growth.*

'Ah, see,' I said, 'but you're not an animal.'

He smirked. 'That's not what you said last night.'

I pulled a coy smile, which I dropped at the sight of the test stick on the dresser from yesterday. I must have stood for a few moments, listening to my thoughts. It was the same ovulation test I'd taken for the last year, after months of trying and failing to conceive. I would need to restock from our local pharmacy, once again bracing myself for dear Mr Sharma, the pharmacist, and his excessively sympathetic smile. He'd even started offering advice and recommending supplements with a certain forced indifference, unable as he did so to look me in the eyes. Like the time he stood right beside me in the aisle, examining and aligning items on the shelves as he surreptitiously (eyes remaining forward) handed me a box of vitamins, palm down like a bribe.

Gabe was oblivious of my meandering thoughts, his eyes focusing again on his phone. 'I've got an early start. Meeting with John and Sophie,' he said, swinging himself out of bed. John was Gabe's supervisor for his PhD in astrophysics and cosmology at King's College London, who believed arriving on time meant you were already late and taking holidays was an admission of weakness. Sophie was his uncomfortably attractive research assistant, with whom he was compelled (so he said) to spend an inordinate amount of time.

Grabbing and holding up my book, which was a permanent fixture on my nightstand, he playfully tugged at my towel. 'Should I be jealous of this Brilliant Savoury chap?' he said.

I pushed him away, ignoring the question on my mind: *Should I be jealous of Sophie?*

'First, his name is Jean Brillat-Savarin,' I said, taking the book from him, 'and no, because he's been dead for like two hundred years.' Gabe was clearly intelligent, but I'd often wondered if there was only a fine line between intelligence and stupidity, a bit like the relationship between genius and insanity.

'Okay,' he said, 'I accept I'm better at the eating part of the art of cookery.'

'Hasn't gone unnoticed,' I replied.

Gabe rubbed his face, then stared at the carpet.

'Ads,' he said, 'did you do a headstand last night? In bed?'

I blanked my face. 'No. Why would I do that?'

'Hmm. Strange dream, I guess. Anyway, have a great day at cook school, Addy-girl,' he said. 'Be good, and don't worry about me. Your dinner with a bunch of wannabe chefs is bound to be epic. See you around midnight. Oh, and remember, I'll be late back tomorrow night.'

'Again?'

'That Sophie's got me running around.'

Even thinking of her couldn't steal my joy today. I smiled a manic, toothy grin as he left the room. Gabe often worked late with colleagues and it would normally be me waiting around for his return. Tonight, he'd be waiting for me. But the best thing was that Le Cordon Bleu had taken my mind off the anxiety of our fertility challenges, at least for a while.

## 8.30am

As I hopped down the stairs, I paused in our hall. I could tell from the strength of Gabe's scent that he had paused there too, which made sense because of our Wisdom Wall. It had started with a plaque Gabe had bought for me. Silver words on driftwood read, *The belly rules the mind. Spanish proverb.* He couldn't have known the significance of that simple gift, or how for just a moment I'd wondered if he knew the secret Nana and I shared about what our recipes could do. And then, from me to him, arrived another plaque, in the shape of a pan, which made him laugh so much we gave it prime position in the centre of the wall: *I'll bet what motivated the British to* colonise so much of the world is that they were just looking for a decent meal. *Martha Harrison*. Eventually the whole wall was full. There were wisdoms on wood, etched into glass, painted on canvas, nailed, pinned, and even, in the case of *Fake it till you make it*, taped. Sagacious overload, Gabe called it. *Follow your heart, it already knows the way* sat next to *Be who you are*, and hidden down by the skirting board, *The opposite of bravery is not cowardice, but conformity*.

There were times when, as I passed through the hall, my eyes would fall upon a plaque which related to a particular situation I was facing, and the wise words would help in small ways. Like an epigraph for my day.

As I stood in the hall that morning, memories of the previous night lit up my mind. Including how afterwards, when I had thought Gabe was asleep, I had indeed done a headstand, only to tumble off the bed as he asked, in a barely conscious state of slumber, 'What you doing?'

'Yoga,' I had replied without pausing for a beat.

I rested my hand on my belly as I stared out of the window at the clock face of Christ Church, my sphinx clock. *You never know*, I said speaking to the air about me. *Perhaps this month*. I imagined a quickening inside, almost felt it, low in my belly.

*You never know*.

# 5.30pm

Somewhere in between registration, the tasting of samples and the demonstrations, the welcome dinner for students had been cancelled. I was pleased, as it had already been a long day and I was relieved to be going home earlier than planned.

The highlight of the session had been the moment my 'new age' cookery tutor, Celine, wearing a bandana and maroon lipstick, sat cross-legged on the floor and seated the class in a circle around her, like shamans around a camp fire. Each student was asked to introduce themselves. Acne-speckled Stephen from Brixton, who spent summers at his dad's restaurant, which sounded like a takeaway; Linda from Islington, who went crimson as she spoke and who loved to bake. Then after two others, my turn arrived. I am naturally shy, although had you met me you might never have realised, because years ago I'd learned the art of hiding it in public spaces. The trick was to go loud. Being as brash and vivacious as I could operated as a temporary cure. No-one would guess I was shy. That said, it did take great resolve to do what I did next. Standing for enhanced impact, and fighting my nerves, I spoke.

'Hello, everyone,' I had said with theatrical confidence. 'My name is Addy – Audrey – Mayford, and I'm from London. I'm also married (*big 'so there' smile*) to a gorgeous man called Gabriel – we've no children . . . yet, but we're working on that (*suggestive chuckle, raised eyebrows*). I'm here because I've always wanted to become a chef. Since I could stand, I've cooked with my Nana every day. First, standing on dining chairs to reach the worktop, then on a low stool, and finally on my tippy toes. Still do that now, actually!' There were a few snickers around the circle as I tapped my head to indicate my height. 'Over the years, Nana taught me ancient recipes that were handed down through generations, and my Nana and her recipes are my inspiration. My wonderful husband – who by the way is gorgeous . . . did I say that already? – supports me one hundred percent.'

Murmurs had trickled in a low volume: 'Wow – wonderful', 'Sounds amazing' and also, in a just about audible whisper, 'F-ing Stepford wife'.

'I know, I know. I am lucky,' I'd said, smoothing a frown and speaking as loudly as I reasonably could in defiance of the whisperer, 'but I do appreciate it all. I know how blessed I am, trust me (*wide smile*), and I must say I am so excited to be here . . .' I flailed my arms around with a big, bordering-on-hysterical grin on my face, 'to be enhancing my cookery skills at such a prestigious establishment.'

What a smug bitch I must have seemed.

# 6.00pm

When I approached home, Christ Church sat on its haunches, resplendent, the rays of a golden sunset rebounding off its walls. The streets glowed in the way only a city can, with sunlight striking off so many surfaces. Gabe wouldn't be home for a couple of hours yet. The day was high and blue, with the scent of damp leaves in the air. In the distance, I could hear the hum of a propeller aeroplane, which seemed odd; I associated their buzz, like bees and flies, with hot summer days. As a meticulous planner, I had adjusted my schedule immediately on the cancellation of the restaurant plans, but the bright afternoon had made me disinclined to follow through. It had been my intention to cook Don't Be Sad Spinach and Lamb, which I'd been making a lot recently. It is a deeply flavoursome and mouthwatering dish, featuring amongst my favourites, and is best eaten with freshly cooked chapatis. I always liked to place an indulgent curl of butter upon it and eat the meal as the butter melted over the spinach and lamb. But on such a high after my course, it didn't seem like the right dish to prepare that evening.

Next, I walked past my home and on to Spencer Street, which ran adjacent to my street and housed a number of ramshackle shops and eateries, including, squeezed between the disparate commercial offerings, Jim's Corner

Shop – which wasn't on the corner, but between a house and the grocery store, artfully named The Grocery Store. My unplanned diversion meant I could buy an ingredient I needed for the meal I now intended to create for supper. This was also the penultimate dish I had deployed in my mission to win Gabe's love: an uplifting delight, capable of raising joyous feeling to epic heights. As I filled a brown paper bag with taro root, the dish's key ingredient, the sight of this unusual vegetable, which has the appearance of a small, dark, hairy ball, brought to mind my visit the previous week to the fertility clinic.

It's funny how trying to have a child had taken over my life. How, at the age of only twenty, I should have to visit a fertility clinic. I never expected to feel like such a failure, so let down by a body that wouldn't do what evolution intended. I knew I had all these other things going for me – great husband, loving family – but at times, it all felt like nothing. Sometimes I felt as if my insides were not made up of organs and tissues, but of sugar cubes, and every month the failure to conceive melted a bit of me away. One touch and what remained of me would crumble, though those sugar cubes grew strong again when I was cooking or writing recipes. In those times, I would feel as if nothing was wrong.

My appointment at the fertility clinic the previous week had been to collect the results of our recent tests. Gabe had an important meeting with his PhD supervisor so couldn't attend. The waiting room had the appearance of a domestic living room, with an oversized coffee table in the centre. The magazines on the table were a scattered mess, so I organised them, placing them into date and size order, oldest and largest at the bottom. I'd read most of them at least twice anyway, due to all the tests we'd had to come for since signing up.

'Ms Mayford.' The voice came from a thin, orange-coloured girl with bleached blonde hair and white overalls. She reminded me of the girl who'd handed me a form entitled Personal Questionnaire when we first signed up at this clinic, requiring me to tick a box to indicate whether I was black, white, Chinese, Asian. This filled me with dread because there was no tick box for me. There never was. Memories of my challenging schooldays flooded back. Eventually, after much deliberation, I had ticked white and handed the form back to the waiting girl, who had given me a quizzical look.

The new girl had the look of a mature fourteen-year-old. I always wondered why they hired such young girls to work here. They'd clearly never been pregnant and sometimes, observing their finger-thinness, I wondered if menses were even a part of their lives yet.

'Hello, I'm Chloe,' she said. 'You're here for Dr Gloucester?'

I nodded. I had become attached to Dr Gloucester. She

had for me become an expert, confidante and friend rolled into one.

'Only Dr Gloucester's still in a meeting at the moment.' Chloe was aggressively sympathetic, the way the staff here were, head tipped to one side, brows raised. 'If you like I can see if Felicity's available to see you.'

Felicity was one of the older nurses, with ample hips, and she had my file open on screen as I walked in. As I sat, she hit a button to blacken the screen.

'Addy,' she said, greeting me. Felicity was grey-blonde with flushed skin, which gave her the look of someone who'd just returned from a jog. 'We've got your results back.'

'Finally,' I said.

'Let me just get them up.'

'Actually, I was wondering if I might be pregnant,' I said while she was scrolling down the screen, 'because I've been feeling these twinges.'

'I see from your notes you've had these sensations before, love . . . a few times.'

'But this time it's different – it's more intense and . . .' I took a moment. 'Well, there's this thing I've been doing, after we . . . it's a bit like a headstand . . . it's supposed to help the sperm to—'

'Ah . . . I see.'

'Umm, gravity,' I finished lamely. There was an awkward pause.

'Hmm,' she hummed. The choral performance then came to an abrupt halt as Felicity turned to look at me square. For the shortest moment, I saw a look in her eyes. A tightening, like the sensation of pain. And then it was gone. Exchanged for a forced smile, a stretching of lips.

'We don't generally suggest such approaches, Addy. They're mostly old wives' tales.'

I took a moment to consider this. 'So is there any way of telling if . . .' I said, leaving my sentence incomplete.

'No, not around ovulation.' She picked up her pen, started fidgeting with it. 'You have to wait until nearer the end of the month. No test in the world can tell you you're pregnant around the moment of conception.'

My mouth formed a pout. I'd been about to ask about Qi Gong, a sort of yoga for fertility I'd read about, but I decided to hold back, to curtail Felicity's evidently growing suspicions that I was mental.

'Anyway, the results. I'm afraid things don't look good. We've collated all the investigative test results, yours and Gabe's, and . . .' Felicity placed her hand upon my arm, 'it looks unlikely that you will ever have children of your own.'

She carried on speaking. I nodded, as if she was talking about the weather. Inside, my stomach knotted into a great weight. *Breathe, Addy*, I told myself. *Breathe.* Disjointed words like *unexplained* and *ovarian* and *failure* bounced off the walls.

'Can I suggest we arrange another meeting? With you and your husband. It's better that the doctor explains it to you both in detail.'

I heard myself say, 'Yes,' although it was as if someone else was speaking.

I stood, steadying myself against a wall. Then I left the clinic swiftly, head down, to avoid the rehearsed, aggressive sympathy of the three reception staff near the exit.

That night, Gabe and I had stared at the wall for an hour, not speaking a word.

The next day, we carried on with life as if nothing had happened.

I shook the memory away as I headed home, little knowing Gabe would be there. Two hours early.

In bed.

The smell of sweat hanging in the air and the wardrobe door I'd left open now tightly shut.

# 8

# Make it Better Tea Rice (*page 31*)

For the soul to be healed and uplifted, take:

1 onion, sliced and fried
6 cloves garlic, minced
240g tin chick peas
250g yogurt
2 tsp cumin seeds
2 large black cardamoms, cracked
5cm/2in cinnamon stick
6 cloves
1 tsp peppercorns
salt to taste
2 cups basmati rice

The taste: a subtly flavourful infusion.
The artistry: to show that gentleness and patience can
lead to great things. Not everything need be big and bold
and strongly flavoured for magic to work.
The purpose: to remind you of the good things in life and
infuse you with quiet contentment.

THE DAY AFTER I FOUND GABE NAKED IN BED AT 6.15PM for no obvious reason, I went to see Nana.

'Addy, how are you, *beti*? Come have tea.' Nana acted surprised to see me, but the kettle was on and my mug, the one I always used with the sparrows on it, was out beside hers with a teaspoon inside. I'd stopped marvelling at her premonitory abilities years ago. In the background she was playing the ABBA song 'Mamma Mia'. Her taste in music went between ABBA and the high-pitched warble of long-dead singers of the subcontinent, such as Lata Mangeshkar, stopping nowhere in between. ABBA was the only Western music that resonated with her, which, she says, is 'sweet on the ears, like Lata'. She kissed me on the forehead. I could smell the mellow scent of yogurt infused with garlic and onion bubbling on the hob.

'I'm fine. Just missing you, Nana,' I said. I didn't tell

her anything of my fears and suspicions about Gabe.

'I'm cooking Make it Better Tea Rice for you, *beta*, one of your favourites,' she said, her knowing eyes jumping about my face.

Nana placed the rice in the savoury, yogurty base and whispered into the bubbling broth, casting her wishes upon it with a gentle blow. And then she poured water from the kettle into our mugs with the teabags. I had a warm sensation of calm familiarity wash over me, the anticipation and luscious scent of the dish already working its magic. I thought about the entry for this in my Ms Mayford recipe book:

Apart from its life-changing qualities, if you can make a cup of tea, you can make this dish. The principle is the same: infusion. Whereas you steep a teabag in boiling water, for this you steep a selection of whole, unground spices (cumin, cinnamon, big black cardamom, cloves and whole black peppercorns) in a base of fried onion and garlic with yogurt, salt and a tin of chick peas. After it's 'brewed', just add boiling water in an approximate measure for the basmati rice to cook. Not so different from brewing a pot of tea. And it only gets better the next day, even if cold, when a different quality of flavour emerges.

But I couldn't eat. Not a single bite.

'Addy,' Nana said. 'What's wrong?'

'Nothing, Nana,' I lied as I took a sip of tea. How could I tell her I feared Gabe was being unfaithful? She came over to me and ran her hand over my head.

'Remember, Addy,' she said. 'Nothing that hits you was ever going to miss you. Nothing that misses you was ever going to hit you.'

Later that evening, back in our flat, Gabe comes home from work late and tells me he is leaving me, his words spoken in the tone of voice normally used to tell me he is planning to get milk from our local Tesco Metro. I don't realise he's leaving immediately. He mumbles something about needing space, that he isn't sure any more, that he needs time to think. His words are like the lyrics of a million sad love songs; I know their melodies, know how they go. But I cannot grasp the meaning. Slowly they form, reform, then settle.

I repeat his phrases in a whisper, follow him upstairs and watch him pack. Then something within me breaks and spills.

Gabe is silent as I confront him. He is silent as I rail, his eyes never meeting mine. I move swiftly from fury to businesslike reasoning, as if I can argue him out of leaving. Professional words that seem as tasteless as paper. And when that fails, to my shame, I plead, beg. Finally, I accuse: *There's someone else, isn't there?*

He pauses for a moment. Looks at me, then drops his eyes to the floor.

'There is no-one else, Addy,' he says. And then instead of continuing to pack, he sweeps up his half-full duffle bag and takes the stairs in three strides.

He stops in the hall before our wedding photos, holds my favourite picture up, stroking the image of my face as if I'm not right there with him.

He drops the photograph in his bag, then pulls at the door.

And I know, in that moment, I will never see him again.

'Gabe,' I say, in a whisper, my breath jolting. He pauses, hand on the open door. 'There's something I have to say.'

For the first time, his eyes meet mine. He's crying, his face stiff, lips tight as if to contain something. 'You have given me the purest joy I've ever known . . . and . . .' I trail off.

He dips his head, eyes lowered, the silence for those few beats like a prayer. 'Addy, I . . .' he says. And then nothing. He leaves. Walks away until he's shrunk into a full stop in the distance. Then he vanishes into the dark night, not pausing once to glance back. Gabe. Gone. Like a story lost to history, never to be told again.

\* \* \*

And that thought, with everything that has passed, sends me to bed.

Too sad to cry, too shocked to think. My recipes a distant memory. I cannot sleep. I lie like the dead, staring. The moon's a perfect orb framed by our bedroom window. I turn to my left, to Gabe. I want to show him. Only he's not there. I reach up to it, imagining its cool surface. So beautiful and yet so far away; too far to ever touch, like the life I once had.

I'd never given it much thought until now, but I had always been fairly certain residents of hell are denied access to fresh food and health-giving provisions as their punishment. Hell is real, of course, whether Dante's, the Bible's, or the Quran's, but I'd always believed it to be a fiery pit where the wicked, hateful and murderous are flung to be tormented by grotesque, half-human beasts. Residents are subjected to sensory deprivation, while fed a single repeat menu of tepid baked beans on economy white bread, surrounded by the scent of motorway service station deep-fryer grease as they are taunted and ridiculed to the sound of incessant, torturous wailing. Unthinkable misery, to my mind.

Now I realise hell isn't all that.

Hell is simple.

It's separation. From truth. From love. From people. Your people, when they walk away.

And the residents of hell are those left behind.

Me.

The decline over the next few days was rapid. Exponential. Sleepless. My eyes white and wide through the night. I stayed in bed and, despite a grating hunger, couldn't eat. With high fever I fell into that pit of bottomless grief visited by so many before me: the cheated, the abused, the betrayed. And even though he'd denied it, still I suspected there was someone else.

Not knowing why Gabe had left subjected me to a peculiar kind of torture, slowly morphing from that darkening pinprick of despair every day until it resembled a gaping black hole. And black holes – the interstellar variety – were to my mind a good metaphor for the way my whole existence had collapsed into nothingness.

# AFTER . . .

# 9

# Stay Strong Chicken Yakhni Soup
## (*page 33*)

For patience and constancy, leading to inner strength, take:

1 onion, sliced
1 big black cardamom
4cm/2in cinnamon stick
1 tsp coriander seeds
1 tsp cumin seeds
4 cloves
10 black peppercorns
4 cloves garlic, minced
1 tsp ginger, finely chopped
6 chicken pieces
a dash of turmeric powder
1 chicken stock cube, dissolved in boiling water
a touch of salt

The *taste*: clear and silky with a resonating yet subtle flavour.

The *artistry*: to extract the essence of things, less being at times so much more.

The *purpose*: to lead you through the thorny forest of hurt, bestowing patience and constancy to strengthen your heart.

I WANTED THE SLEEP OF THE ANCIENTS. LIFE-CHANGING sleep.

Years ago, Nana told me a story about young men who slept their way out of trouble. The story of the People of the Cave. Mum, when she heard it, said Nana meant the Seven Sleepers of Ephesus. An argument broke out, which I defused by saying numbers and names didn't matter; they were both right. It was the same story, told two ways.

The story tells of a group of young men who hid inside a cave with their dog, Rakim, to escape persecution for refusing to pray to anything other than God. Only, Sleeping-Beauty-like, they stayed many years in a deep, mysterious slumber, Rakim keeping watch over them. When they woke, they were certain they'd only been asleep for a day or so. One of them went to buy food and discovered the truth. Their coins had been out of circulation for hundreds of years. Legend has it that some of them kept growing when asleep and ended up becoming giants, now buried in four-metre-long graves.

I wanted to sleep my way to a different time and place (my height I was content with). And so, I stayed in bed and slept. And when I couldn't sleep, I'd regress into memories of my childhood, living in a past long gone. Broken images came: Jen, the bullies, a large arc of blue sky smudged with white clouds, teachers, the scent of cut grass and that time, many years ago, when I'd gone with Nana to Lahore. I could smell the garlands; the warm air of a foreign land; family members who were strangers to me holding me in an urgent embrace, as if I was someone returned who'd been missing for years.

The next few days happened in snatches.

The place was a mess, my diet consisting of things microwaved or removed from tins. Then one day Nana arrived at the door. She didn't say anything but instead comforted me like a toddler who'd taken a tumble. Tuts and hums and strokes. She sat beside me, whispering prayers under her breath, silent and ghostly. After a couple of days I realised she'd as good as moved in, making her bed on the couch. Every day she fed me Stay Strong Chicken Yakhni Soup. I remember her flesh, soft as down pillows, and our heads lightly touching, like when I was a child.

Then Mum arrived. She stopped abruptly when she saw me. I could see she was nervous as she reached forward to hand me something in a brown paper bag. There were tears quivering in the corners of her eyes. I pulled it out. A Jamie Oliver cookbook. I was crying then, couldn't stop, because I felt Mum's love in that simple gift. Mum, who always said don't waste your life on cookery. She walked over, her arms wide, and held me in a tight embrace. I was a child again, buried in her arms as something cracked and spilt. And I told her everything.

Jen came round and we were left alone together in the bedroom. I could tell she was worried about me. She began to cry, becoming inconsolable as she eyed me in a fetal curl under the covers in the daytime.

'Jen,' I said, 'I'm fine. I'll be fine. Don't worry.'

But she moved to full-blown hysterics. It took some time to settle her down. Wasn't she meant to be consoling me? And yet here I was comforting her. It just showed how much she felt for me.

'Jesus, Jen,' I said, 'this is beyond the call. There, there,' I said, stroking her hair. 'Calm down. I'm fine, really. I'll be fine.'

Later that day, I was on the sofa with a cup of tea.

'Addy, *beta*, I have been thinking,' Nana said. 'It's time you went to Lahore. It's time you met your . . .' she paused, then continued, 'your relatives there.'

'Why would I go there, Nana? That place is nothing to do with me. Everything and everyone I love is here.' I thought of the 'face' I had worn since childhood. Since I'd realised people saw me as different when I was at school. It was the part of my heritage that had only caused me strife. And since I had successfully hidden it away, why would I exhume it now?

And then I thought of Dad. The fond memories of the time I visited Lahore as a child. Emotions crashed against each other. I ran my fingers through my hair, wondering if it would have been different if Dad was still alive. I didn't know.

I took a long, slow sip of tea. I couldn't bear the thought of leaving the house, let alone the country. And what if Gabe returned?

'No, Nana. I don't want to go to Lahore. I don't want to go anywhere.'

Nana looked at me, an unreadable expression on her face. 'Addy, *beta*, there was a time that I needed help. More help than our recipes could provide.' She moved closer to me to stroke my hair. 'You remember that time I took you with me to Pakistan. With your father,' she said. 'I never told you, you were so young, but I was there for a reason. Things were bad, so bad between your Mum and Dad. It was too much for me. And that's why I went to Lahore, to the Wishing Place. I wanted to put things right.'

'Wishing Place?'

'It's a place called Data Darbar, the burial place of a saint called Data Ganj Baksh. They say prayers to God offered there are always answered. Millions go, but in all my life, I only went during that time in Lahore with you. You see, Addy, there is a belief about saints, *walis*, *Pirs*, the 'friends' of God. That they are so blessed that their blessedness spills out and spreads like a great cloud engulfing the air, sky and earth about them, even after death. Miraculous favours can land upon anyone, simply by being in that vicinity. People say if you pray to God in such blessed places your wishes are always granted. And so I went there to pray.'

'For Mum and Dad to get back together?'

'No,' Nana said. She paused, looking me in the eye. Took my hand. 'I went for you, Addy. It was for you. To pray that you would not be abandoned by your Dad the way he had been, that you would grow up with both your parents around.'

She told me that this was why she had come back to London, even though Mum and Dad had split up. I was her charge, her responsibility. And she would not abandon me, even if Dad had. She told me her greatest fear when Dad left was that she'd be forcibly separated from me as a result. Mum, bitter and angry, wanted nothing to do with her or Dad, but in the end Nana had struck a deal to be able to stay in Mum's house. They would share the task of raising me. But there were rules. And Nana had no choice but to agree. As to what those rules were, she wouldn't say.

Jen came to visit again. Nana was downstairs cooking in the kitchen.

'Nana's arranged it all,' Jen said. 'It's all been planned.'

'What's that?'

'You and I are going to Lahore.'

I yawned. 'I'm tired,' I said. 'I'm not going anywhere.' I turned away, buried my head in a pillow. I had to be here in case Gabe finally returned one of my calls or texts, or even came home.

'Come on, Ads. We'll be like students on a gap year. Only for ten days, because that's all the leave entitlement I've got left at work.'

'We're not students, Jenny,' I said, 'and I'm not ready yet to go anywhere. You go. Take someone else.' I pretended to be falling asleep.

I heard shuffling. Jen started removing clothes from my wardrobe, folding them into a case. 'Too late, Ads. It's been arranged. Booked and paid for. You need a break, and Nana's arranged for me to take you to see your relatives. They're expecting us and we're leaving tomorrow.'

'What?' I said, with a rise of annoyance. It felt good. To feel. 'Leave those alone,' I said.

She stopped. There was a face-off for a beat or two and then her features began to contort. The thought of her breaking down on me again was unbearable. I closed my eyes.

'I'll do it,' I said, defeated. 'I'll pack.'

'Good,' she said smiling, 'you stubborn cow.' I didn't tell her the reason I'd changed my mind. That I was thinking of the Wishing Place Nana had told me about. Nana had been there once in her time of great need. And I would go there now, to petition the Lord for my own salvation.

When Mum found out I was going to Lahore, she was straight on the phone, and a tirade followed. She called it madness, told me I couldn't go, said that Pakistan wasn't safe. 'That Nana of yours, just you wait till I speak to her,' she said. This seemed very strange because in the past, other than her urging me to pursue a lucrative career (or any career other than cookery), Mum had never taken much of an interest in anything I did.

'Mum, I didn't even want to go . . .'

'So don't!'

'It's all booked. And anyway, I've nothing else to do.'

'Listen, Addy, I forbid you to go.'

'Mum, please. I can make up my own mind.'

She hung up. I put the phone down, confused by the

exchange, but dismissed it. Perhaps Mum was just in a bad mood. I was sure it would pass.

The morning dawned with us packed and ready when Jen told me she had a surprise. I thought of cuddly toys or Snickers bars. But no. When she opened the front door for us to leave, there was Nana in the doorway, Dr Martens under a floaty silk sari, toast-coloured skin exposed at her midriff. On the pavement, a buckled soft suitcase, and slung over her shoulder, a sheet, balled like something carried by a character from a nursery rhyme.

'Nana's coming too!' Jen said.

I smiled in disbelief. The furthest Nana had gone in ten years was the Tesco Metro, a full thirty minutes away by foot; the idea of a holiday or travelling anywhere abroad was ludicrous to her. She didn't even do summer holidays to Cornwall. And now, this? It showed me just how much she loved me.

So we set off, Nana, Jen and I, three adventurers on our way to Heathrow Airport, Terminal 3, to travel to the faraway lands of my ancestors and, in my case at least, to petition the Lord to change my life.

As soon as I had accepted that we were actually going, I'd written a letter to Gabe and posted it to his office.

Dear Gabe,

I am writing to you because I am leaving for Pakistan. Nana thinks I need to get away and so Jen and I are going to stay with family there. I am not sure why I'm writing this, because we haven't spoken since the day you left, and I don't even know if you want to speak to me or even if you'll get this. You haven't returned my calls or texts. But I have to write, even though I don't know where to begin.

Perhaps I should start with the things I never told you. Things I think I should have. Not because I was keeping them from you, but because it's hard to say such things between the mundane activities in everyday life. How can you pause loading a dishwasher to proclaim the deep and meaningful to the love of your life?

The good thing is, though, in this letter, I think I can.

I keep thinking of the day you said you wanted to marry me. I was so happy, even though I kept you waiting, as if I had to think about it. And the ring. How I wouldn't put it on because I didn't want to ruin it. Sounds mad to say now, since it's been covered with dough, oil and Fairy Liquid countless times since then. How much fun it was to announce our engagement to all the stars in the night sky you could name. I think Betelgeuse was your best address!

I meant what I said the day you walked away. You have given me the purest joy I have ever known. In bed with you on our wedding night that first time, it was so new, so unfamiliar.

The feeling though, Gabe. Do you remember? It was joy that felt like freedom. Pure happiness. And it filled me totally. I could have died then and it really wouldn't have mattered. (About half an hour later though, it would have done ...)

But let me get to the point.

I miss you, Gabe.

I miss you like a limb ripped from my body. And I'm still bleeding. I don't understand anything. If I told you the truth about how I'm coping, you'd probably be worried about me. If you knew, I am sure you would call me or come see me. Perhaps you have a good reason for not contacting me. I just wish you would. Surely you can't just switch off love?

How is it for you? Being apart. Because for me it's painful, literally painful to be in this world without you in my life. I bet you'll think I'm exaggerating. I'm not. It is a physical pain. I could never have imagined it would feel like this. And that's why I mostly try not to be awake.

The point is, I have a request.

Please give me, give us, another chance. I don't care what you did, if there's someone else. And if I am wrong, forgive me for still suspecting. But if there is someone, please just tell me. Not knowing is killing me and I can't imagine what else has happened. And know, Gabe, I forgive you, whatever. I hope you can forgive me, if I've done something wrong. I love you too much and I just want you back.

There is something more I want to say. This is hard, and I

know it will be hard for you too. I guess I have to just come out with it. Gabe, is it that you think we can't have a family? Is that why you left? Because if it is, I don't care what the doctors say, I believe there is still a chance. I have to believe it.

Anyway, if you have ever loved me, if you have the slightest feeling for me still, please get in touch. It would mean so much to me, even if you don't want to be with me. Perhaps it would make it easier for me to accept your decision, and move on, if that's what you want.

I don't know what else to say.

I hope you choose me. Hope and pray.

With all my love,

Squid

# 10

# Despair-Dissolving Mustard Spinach (*page 34*)

For the banishment of despair, so that light can return to your soul, take:

1 onion, sliced finely
3 cloves garlic, crushed
1 tsp garam masala, the five spices of life
1 bowl mustard spinach, boiled and beaten
melted butter, a great wodge of it

The taste: green and savoury.
The artistry: the power of simplicity.
The purpose: to make your spirit soar.

THEY SAY WHEN YOU INTRODUCE A FISH TO A NEW TANK, you must switch off all the lights, let it swim about in the dark. That way, when the darkness lifts, entry into its new world is less of a shock to the system. My arrival in Pakistan was like this, the dark of night allowing me to be gently lowered into this alternative reality. Even then, in the dark, the city bloomed with new sounds and scents. The heat was urgent, everything a busy spin. Porters in brown uniforms clustered like sparrows after a crumb, urging their assistance upon us. People were rushing everywhere, distracted, causing movement in every direction.

The change immediately filled some of the hurting spaces in me, briefly squeezing out those crushing thoughts which I would inevitably then search out again; and what was that most crushing of them? The moment he left? The fact he had still not been in touch despite my – dare I admit how many – calls and texts? I had less time to press the bruises now. No space or time to wallow.

Nana became a whole new person. She unfurled, her eyes wide, pace fast, her speech flowing. There was a crowd waiting for us at the airport gate. Uncle Musa, Aunty Gulu and numerous others were strangers to me, but they had Nana wiping her tears with the end of her sari between endless embraces, and the traditional greeting, *Assalamu-alaikum*, meaning peace be upon you, sounding everywhere.

Nana's family home in the centre of Lahore was a flat-roofed building with a central courtyard. The windows looking into the courtyard were long and large. From the outside you may have wondered if it was an abandoned storage facility. There was nothing to see but blank sandy walls and tired double wooden gates, while every-thing looking inwards was charming, the courtyard laid like a living room with netted day beds, a coffee area, ailing plants in chapped earth struggling to make their presence felt.

We were ushered into the living room as soon as we arrived. Every surface – the sofas, the rug, the wall hanging, the curtains – bore a lively print and yet nothing matched, which, strangely, made it all work together. Only my Uncle Musa and Aunty Gulu lived here. Neither were married. Uncle Musa was tall and square and kept patting me on the head as if I were a member of the *Canis familiaris* species. I immediately noticed the way he moved, the way he flattened the hair at the back of his head, just as I remembered Dad used to. Aunty Gulu, who had a slight limp, presented me with a knitted doll when I arrived and spent the whole evening with her arm linked in mine. She had a wide, innocent smile, chocolate skin that deepened to ebony around her sunken eyes. It didn't take long for me to see that she was different. Child-like still, despite her age.

I was introduced in those early hours to an endless stream of further people: cousins, neighbours and friends, friends of cousins and cousins of friends, with complete strangers dotted between, all at 1.00 in the morning, everyone having stayed up for our arrival. It was too much to take in. Nana was endlessly being wrapped in lengthy embraces, having speedy conversations in Urdu and Panjabi that I barely understood. For some reason, I had never really appreciated that Nana had this other persona with other people and acquaintances in another land. It was only now I could see just how much she had left behind to be with me in London.

Everyone was fascinated by Jen's blonde hair, her bloodless white skin, as if she were a different human specimen, never seen before. The visitors didn't stop. I remember a rotund neighbour with rosy cheeks, claiming some distant kinship for which I couldn't find a word (second cousin twice removed aunt by marriage or something incomprehensible like that), a family with three children, groomed with oiled hair and evidently told to be well behaved as they sat beside each other, staring at each of us in turn. The teenagers all had their hair tied up high or plaited to one side, and introduced themselves as Sweetie, Pinky and Baby. I laughed, thinking this must be a joke, until it became apparent that, no, these were the names they went by. We were like great celebrities, drawing crowds to glimpse us in wonder. At about 2.00 am, an elderly man arrived, the crowd moving aside for him like the parting of Biblical seas. He was ancient, with wet bruise-coloured lips, a long white beard, and hair topped with a flat cap. He had bones for legs and arms covered by crushed brown-paper-bag skin. He mostly nodded, not saying much to Nana, other than, *Tik hai, humshera?* You are well, sister? But every time he did speak, there would be a ripple in the gathering crowd standing round or sitting at his feet. I later discovered he was a *Pir*, a holy man with the force of the mystical about him, and that he was also a hafiz of the Quran, a memoriser who had committed every word of the Holy Book to memory in exact sequence, like Nana. I would discover this to be fairly common practice in Pakistan, although at the time, it was for me still a thing of wonder. With the *Pir* was a young man dressed in a button-down shirt and chinos, his hair falling in soft curls about his face. There was something strange about him. It took me a while to realise that it was his eyes. They looked undercooked, in a world where everyone else's were 'well done'. Mesmerising pale eyes that stood out against the earthy tones of his skin. I had seen those exact eyes before on a poster bearing the image of a startled Afghan girl: turquoise, circumferenced by flecks of pure gold, and finished with a circle of lapis lazuli. He had the look of a model in *Vogue* magazine and stood a head taller than others in the room. I thought he might be the holy man's son or grandson, the way he took him by the arm when he arrived and led him through the crowds as he left. At this point, everyone got the message and finally, in the early hours of the morning, we retired to our rooms.

Nana and I were sharing one room, while Jen took another. Excitement and exhaustion left us unable to sleep. It was past 3.30 in the morning. People say the early hours are ungodly, but Nana has always said those hours are the most godly of all. I agree. As the world sleeps, I've always felt an eerie magic in the silence. Peace and calm. But now corrosive thoughts of Gabe seep in, and I sink again to that hollow place. The cycle is never-ending; me staring at the darkness with unseeing eyes. Then Gabe appears to me and yet I cannot reach him. He doesn't see me. I am invisible. The missing him is so deep it becomes grief. I think of him dancing his silly dances to *her*, engulfing her in his warm muskiness. Yes, it's grief I feel, as if he'd died. *How was I your everything, and then your nothing, in a single strike?* I hated the love I felt for him, that it tortured me, wouldn't stop and go away.

I realise Nana is watching me, her eyes glinting in the dark. I smile my widest smile, even though I really want to cry. *Mustn't show her*, I think.

'Addy,' Nana says, 'I know.' That's all. For a while she says nothing more, just strokes my forehead with her thumb, hand resting warm upon my head. What does she mean?

'You think of me as tough and strong and wonderful,' she says. 'And it's true, I am.' She smiles a one-sided smile. 'But I have also seen terrible things, just like you. I know your suffering. My child, listen to what I tell you now; there will be more, tsk.' She clucks, then lightly shakes her head. 'And you must learn to accept terrible things as God's will.'

I cannot say anything for the swelling in my throat. And so I smile again, wider now, to push the tears back in.

'Why did this happen to me, Nana?' I say in a whisper.

'Addy,' Nana says, wiping away a tear with her fingertips, 'let it go, my child. Who can say what God has planned and why?' She takes a deep breath. 'I will show you things, tell you stories of my life that I have never shared before. And you must listen, you must learn. Questions demand answers and I know you have many spinning in your head. But relax. Don't push. Hold them inside, my child, until the answers come to you. And they will. When you pay no mind to them, that's when the answers come.'

I nod.

'And of one thing be sure. Everything is exactly as it should be.'

I don't know what Nana means. Nor do I care. Because what I do know in that moment is that home is not a place. There in Lahore, in the deepest part of the night, thousands of miles from all I know, with Nana I am home.

I awake to the singing of azan, the pre-dawn call to prayer. An ethereal whisper carries on the air, like the exhale of Nana's breath upon my face.

'Nana,' I say, nudging her as she sleeps, 'will you take me to the Wishing Place?'

She grunts out a yes, turns and whistles back to sleep.

The next morning, before breakfast, Aunty Gulu took Jen and me on a tour of the residence, walking us through rooms designed to block the punishing sun and keep insects out. Mesh screens clouded every window, floors were cold, off-white stone, walls rough-plastered and bare, and faded dhurrie rugs, thin and handwoven, lay scattered on the floor here and there. The rooms had a frugal charm, housing only the essentials. Some rooms connected; others, mostly padlocked, could be entered only via the courtyard.

At first, there was no talk of going anywhere and we didn't do much but chat, rest and receive visitors. The slower pace of life pressed down upon us, until we realised there was no choice but to succumb. Nothing was rushed; life itself was conspiring to amble us along at its own gentle pace. Eventually, like wading through water, I gave in to it. Yet somehow it helped to do so. After those first few days, the world seemed different. It's true, I was up and down. But moment to moment, there were more ups than downs.

Even before seeing much, Lahore was like a loud beautiful noise in my ears, drowning out my misery. I swung from dark, depressive moods to moments of levity, at times even within reach of joy. It was amazing to me how quickly a new environment, new people, a new country could change my outlook, almost inappropriately so, given that I had, after all, lost the love of my life. Should I not remain permanently immersed in a dark hole of misery? But if you ignored the dead of night, you could say I had begun to mend.

Nights, though, remained the worst. When alone with my thoughts and memories, the old dark, brooding me was always at risk of resurfacing.

Soon we'd rested and recovered from the journey, and the visitors had thankfully petered out. When a risk of a resurgence threatened, we gained a robustness, an ability to feign alternative pre-arranged engagements at will, so that they hesitated and promised to come back another time.

I knew my holiday had begun in earnest when we were all gathered around, staring at a bowl of spinach issuing a celestial scent.

'Addy, *beta*, you must try this,' said Uncle Musa, who had brought in the dish Nana had just made, and we all stood in admiration, as if it was something recently birthed, like a baby or a kitten. The day before, Nana had taken Jen and me to Lahore Fort. We had lingered, enthralled, as we watched a pink sunset over the exotic battlements, but beautiful though it was, it hadn't held our rapt attention to quite the same degree as this bowl of spinach.

We all stood in the dining area, which morphed without any indication of a shift into a living space rammed full of pink sofas. Nana was busy in the kitchen. As we stared, gulping up the scent and the sight, I was taken back to a seminal moment in my life.

'Uncle Musa,' I said, 'I remember the moment I fell in love.'

'With ... um ...' Jen said, not quite getting to the letter G.

'No, no. When I fell in love with *taste*,' I said. 'You know, Uncle, I've always been crazy about Nana's cookery – its art, its science – but I hadn't really understood taste, not until this moment.'

'Tell me, *beta*,' my uncle said.

'Nana, with her boundless energy, asked me one day to take her for a drive. We did this every few days after I passed my test. It was a relief to leave the congestion of London and take in fresh air, especially when the sky was high and blue. Quite soon, on either side of the loopy, cotton-thread road – the sort where cars have to drive single file – was a patchwork of multi-coloured fields. Driving these roads was life-threatening because there was no way to be warned of oncoming traffic.

'I was driving at a steady twenty miles per hour (in mortal fear of a collision) when Nana, without warning, slapped the dashboard with flat palms and shouted, "Stop!" I slammed on the emergency brake and looked intently for signs of an oncoming vehicle. There was nothing – the road remained a lonely stretch. Nana, shrouded in her regular air of mystery, and providing no explanation, stepped out of the car. She walked unsteadily across the road, her baggy shalwar trousers flapping in the breeze, and climbed the small bank to the field on our left, disappearing out of sight. When she reappeared, she bore a wide betel-leaf-stained grin and an armful of weeds. "*Sarson ka saag*," she said, staring back at me and clucking twice (which generally meant she was pleased). The weeds were leafy, low and dark and resembled the green matter generally heaped into a pile at the end of a garden for later disposal or incineration.

'She crouched down again in the next field, with the ease only those practised at working low to the ground can. I left the car, and approached her, keeping a guilty eye out for a farmer in case he might be nearby. The scented summer day exhaled over my skin and the sunshine blazed its warmth through my hair. The expansiveness was endless. The sight of Nana crouching in the field would have looked more natural in rural India, with her effortless squat, baggy clothes and scarf looped around her head. She swayed back to the car in slow wide steps, her scarf undulating softly to the rhythm of her feet, and deposited the weeds on the back seat.

'Back home in our kitchen, Nana pulled mustard spinach leaves off stalks.

'"Addy," she said with a grave look on her face, "you know as a child in Pakistan, we could never pick crops from a farmer's field."

'"Similar rules apply here," I replied, giving Nana The Look. "I believe the term for it is theft." She clucked dismissively from the side of her mouth as she plucked the leaves from their stalks and told me about the dish she would prepare.

'"The preparation is easy, which is why the magic of

the dish itself is a mystery. But its purpose is that all art requires effort because the magic comes not from the salt and chilli or onion (those ingredients find their way into many a meal) but from the effort that is needed in the final preparation. Quite a pounding is required to meld this dish into a smooth, creamy consistency. Art is at times laborious." (She added a warning that the use of an electric blender is completely out of the question.)

'Nana made a simple bowl of what looked like creamed spinach. But this dish was totally unlike the spinach we know; as different as a banana is from sand. I remember it being deep and creamy and savoury with a subtle undertone of tang. It tasted of green fields in springtime with the scent of sunshine on earth after a rain shower. I named it Despair-Dissolving Mustard Spinach. In my cookery book I placed an entry at page 34 under "Despair and Devastation":

'Though simple and humble in appearance, when raised to the mouth it induces something meditative, virtually ethereal, which cannot fail to infuse you with a deep resonating calm, moving you in small steps towards lifting despair. Savoury, buttery, tangy and deep. This is a simple dish, but never forget that the hallmark of the best art is simple.'

Back in Lahore, the nan bread arrived.

'Can you believe it, Uncle, Jen?' I said. 'Here is the actual dish before us, made by Nana!'

But both Jen and Uncle Musa were too busy pulling at the nan and scooping up the spinach from their plates as I spoke, lost in the glory of taste as I knew they would be. After starting to eat this remarkable meal myself, I began to notice a discernible shift. I found myself positively swimming in a sea of calming butters and savoury greenness, and small shards of light began to penetrate the despair that had taken over my life.

As I bathed in the glow, I could hardly wait for the next day. Nana was finally going to take us to the Wishing Place, the world-famous Data Darbar, the reason I had agreed to come to Lahore in the first place.

# 11

# Serenity Flatbread (*page 38*)

For comfort and warmth, leading to deep calm, take:

250g wholemeal flour
water, as needed, and a dash of oil, to make a dough
butter - a great wodge of it
maple syrup and extra butter, melted

The taste: warm, soft and buttery, like love on the tongue.
The artistry: the power of hands at work.
The purpose: for comfort and calm, like a long hug, to
transform you steadily to serenity.

AT THE FAR SIDE OF THE COURTYARD WAS A ROOM locked with a giant padlock, and the next morning Jen and I were busy inspecting it when Aunty Gulu appeared.

'What's in here?' I said.

'We don't go in there,' Aunty Gulu said with worry in her eyes. 'A djinn baba lives there.' This she said as though she were talking about an unfriendly neighbour.

'A djinn?' Jen repeated. 'Like in Aladdin's lamp?'

Aunty Gulu nodded furiously. 'That's why it's locked. We don't go in there.'

This was no surprise to me. I had heard Nana speak about djinn countless times in this way, as if they were real. I began a lengthy explanation for Jen, starting with the fact they are often mistaken for ghosts and that they are largely invisible beings that reside amongst us, although in a different realm. Their presence, if not seen, can be detected by the feeling of a great wave of heat, or a rising chill, the tell-tale sign being that there is no obvious environmental explanation. The djinn, I continued, are not based on clay, like us, but are made of smokeless fire. And since it is possible to be burned both by great heat and great cold, you feel either a burning or a freezing. Other facts about these fiery folk are that there are different kinds. The powerful and the ordinary, an ifrit being the most powerful of all. Just as there are good and bad amongst humans, likewise there are good and bad djinn folk, but a greater proportion are bad. These are called the Evil Whisperers. It's in the nature of these beings to tend towards evil, in the same way that it's in the nature of wolves to hunt. But most significant of all, the Shaitan, also known as Satan, is from amongst them.

'That's right,' I said. 'Satan is a djinn, not a fallen angel, and he, being endowed with the gift of free will, committed that lesser-known original sin of arrogance when he refused to honour Adam, thinking himself better.'

Jen stepped back from the door. Aunty Gulu and I followed, all of us distancing ourselves from the padlocked room.

'Load of rubbish,' Jen said as she backed away, her eyes widening. 'I don't believe it.'

Aunty Gulu was called away for some errand and Jen and I sat on a *charpai*, a rope hammock bed, and looked up to enjoy the warmth of morning sun on our faces. We must have sat there a while, listening to the sounds of a trader selling their wares in the street, children chasing each other, cars revving and honking in the distance.

'You're feeling better now, aren't you, Ads?' Anxiety distorted Jen's face as she inspected me, while rubbing on layer after layer of her favourite cocoa-butter hand cream. How blessed I was to have such a caring friend; so often she seemed as upset as me about the whole thing.

'Yes, Lahore is definitely helping. Anyway, I think I might know why Gabe left, and I've accepted it.' Jen's eyes, pale and grey, shot me a startled glance. My words around Gabe to date had tended to be rhetorical wails of lament. This was calm, measured.

'Did I tell you, Jen, I'm convinced he's seeing someone else?'

'No, you've not told me anything really, Addy.'

I said nothing more for some while, even though I could feel the force of her curiosity. There were clangs from the kitchen which looked into the courtyard, along with a rising scent of heated dough. Breakfast was being cooked. I watched a cluster of ants in a star formation morph and pulse about a crumb.

'I think Gabe may be seeing someone at his office,' I said.

'No.' Jen gasped in disbelief, just as we were called to breakfast. She didn't push for more information as we sat around the table. I respected that about her. She knew when to stop.

The Serenity Flatbreads, otherwise known as parathas, were some of the best I'd ever tasted. Layers of butter set between leaves of dough, fried and caramelised with sugar. Mouthwatering. Both chewy and crispy at the same time. As soothing as a long hug. I sat calmly staring into the air for some while afterwards, enjoying a mysterious sense of relief, which I knew could only have come from the serenity Nana had kneaded into the dough as she worked.

Just as breakfast finished, Mum called. She sounded worried. How was I? Was everything okay? There wasn't much to tell her yet, so I just tried to allay her fears. Despite this, she kept telling me to come home. I'd never known her so concerned for me. I promised to call again soon.

After a while, I started fiddling with my Dictaphone. I had brought it with me to Lahore because, although my primary aim in coming was to petition God at the Data Darbar, I had decided that since I was going to be here, I could also learn more about my heritage. My reasons for the voice recordings were twofold. I would record my interviews with relatives as they told me all about their lives, especially my Uncle Musa. There would be so much he could tell me about my late father that I would otherwise never come to know, and I wanted to know everything. My secondary secret aim was to improve my language skills, because my command of Urdu was pitiful and my Panjabi non-existent. Most of the younger generation spoke fluent English, the older ones, less so. By recording I could get help translating the many words and phrases that I'd have to pretend to understand while conducting my Q&A sessions with those that didn't speak much English. I didn't want to break their flow with language lessons for myself. As I pressed record to test the machine, I heard Nana calling for some help clearing up the breakfast dishes. And then, shortly afterwards, a deafening scream. Both were caught on my voice recorder.

The scream was one of terror.

I ran into the house to find Aunty Gulu curled on the sofa, looking in horror at the dining table. Approaching her like an injured wild animal, I asked her if she was okay, speaking in my broken mix of English with Urdu words inserted here and there. She spoke back in a similar broken mix, this Urdu-English blend seeming like a whole new language.

'What is it, Aunty, are you hurt?'

She shook her head wildly from right to left, her face squeezed with fear.

'So what is it?' I said, stroking her arm. She pointed at the table. There was nothing on it but a damp cloth.

I went over and lifted it. Aunty Gulu covered her head with her arms. 'Is it this?' I said, holding up the cloth. She nodded. 'What is it?'

She slowly got up.

'*Guria*,' she said, using the pet name coined for me, 'I was cleaning the table and then it . . . it spoke to me!' I raised my eyebrows. 'I show you?'

This was intriguing.

'Okay?'

She pulled the damp cloth back and forth and the cloth against glass emitted a squeaky noise. I could just make out the words, *gul-loo gul-loo*.

'*Ay ya!*' she cried, running back to the sofa and folding herself up again. I struggled to hold back a smile.

'Oh, Gulu, that's just the friction. It's nothing.' She looked relieved as I took her over to the table to reassure her.

Uncle Musa entered the room. 'Is everything okay?' he asked.

I nodded. He smiled at me with such warmth and then told me not to worry about Aunty Gulu and her peculiar ways. He started to gush about how wonderful it was that I'd finally come to see them all in Lahore. He held me in a tight embrace. I left the room with Aunty Gulu looking suspiciously at the cleaning cloth and Uncle Musa smiling adoringly at me.

Aunty Gulu's screams, I was to discover, were a

frequent occurrence. It took very little to terrify her. The next day, as I recall, it was a spider.

Before leaving for the Wishing Place, Nana said we needed to go shopping. Jen put on a shalwar kameez from amongst the many gifts we received on arrival, and a scarf about her neck, and I wore a full-length dress. Jen did a twirl. The long slitted dress and baggy harem-style trousers suited her.

I had imagined a small store, a checkout, the posters in the windows smeared with the blackened glue of last month's, but we stopped at the end of the street little more than twenty paces from our house. A man in dirt-coloured clothing stood behind a single wooden cart, piled impossibly high with fruit and vegetables. Behind him, a glass-eyed ox stood lazily eating scraps of mangled green and brown herbage, its horns high. The streets were alive: people passed with sacks in their arms, on their heads; clay pots under their arms, on their heads; women with children in tow. All a few paces from our home. Kids without shoes wearing oversized, brightly coloured clothing shuffled around us asking for baksheesh. Nana gave them some money, then shooed them away. Instead, more arrived. 'Don't encourage them,' the fruit man said. Nana handed me and Jen some rupees and instructed us to give them out with our palms up. This we dutifully did.

Nana then set about examining the provisions. Prodding tomatoes, turning pawpaws the size of melons about in her hands. She whipped out some sharp words I didn't understand and the trader, like a magician, brought forth more produce from somewhere to the rear of the stall. She made her selection, piece by piece, which I placed in a cloth sack the trader handed me. As she selected, I surreptitiously pointed out bruises and a gash in the pieces she had picked. She dismissed me with a wave of her hand and a cluck. It seemed she was selecting the inferior produce on purpose. She then bargained hard, caved and paid.

We returned home. Aunty Gulu and Nana chopped and peeled until the table was piled high with trays of rainbow-coloured cones: orange, green and red, paw-paw, melon, carrots. And there for lunch, we – Nana, Jen, Uncle Musa, Aunty Gulu and I – ate it all, great high piles of fruit, without a moment's hesitation or reserve. Eating fruit in this quantity, I was to discover, was considered entirely normal in Lahore. Afterwards, Nana went to the kitchen while the rest of us sat in a cosy cluster on the old sofas, nursing our distended stomachs. The sun was high, and through the window its loud light seemed to be shouting. Uncle Musa drew the blinds and came over to me. He laid his hand upon my head, which I had discovered was a thing elders did, a sort of greeting.

'I am so happy you are here. You must see all the great sights in Lahore. I will take you.'

'That would be wonderful, Uncle,' I said.

He stood there a while, smiling at me and nodding, before Nana reappeared. We stood to leave for the Wishing Place, but trailing her were an elderly couple with a young man in tow. We sat down again. I'd discovered quickly that patience and a lack of concern for timing or plans was a necessary minimum to survive Lahore. Neighbours, I guessed, or new long-lost relatives perhaps? The discussion between the elders was animated. The young man in tow edged sideways into the room. He maintained unwavering eye contact with the coffee table, his face lifted in a perma-smile. I couldn't help but notice two diamond-shaped reveals of belly flesh where his shirt was too tight at his midriff, and like a skier trying to look at anything but the flag in the white, I felt my eyes being continually drawn to those flesh diamonds. After an awkward silence, the duty to make polite conversation almost overcame me, but thankfully the desire passed moments later. My full stomach had mildly anaesthetised me and anyway, I didn't like to interrupt whatever he had going on with the coffee table.

In a number of situations, I'd already established I could legitimately claim linguistic ignorance and that was a great help. But I was also unsure of social etiquette. Was I expected to launch into high-spirited conversation or was it okay to sit like a ten-year-old and wait for Nana to finish her tête-à-tête with the elders? By now I had counted six hairs in the upper flesh-diamond and at least a dozen in the lower.

When Nana was finished, they left, and Aunty Gulu brought in more tea. Nana cocked her eyebrows at me and said with a half-smile, 'So. What do you think?'

'Of what?' I replied as I took a gulp of thick masala chai.

'Him, of course,' she said. The tea left my mouth in a magnificent fan-shaped formation. I must have coughed and spluttered for some five minutes, which was only worsened by my failed attempt at covering up the onset of hysterical laughter. I excused myself to the bathroom to release the remaining trapped giggles. I knew then that there had been another undisclosed reason for the visit to Lahore: Nana's attempt to find me a man. A suitable one this time. I hadn't felt such levity in a long while. The idea that I might be compatible with the likes of Midriff Man felt like suggesting I hook up with Donald Duck. Perhaps I would enjoy this holiday more than I already was, I thought.

When I returned from the bathroom, Nana looked miffed at my reaction to her attempted introduction, evidenced by that familiar line between her brows.

'So you didn't like him?' she said.

'It's not that, Nana. I am sure he is very nice.'

'So what then?'

I hesitated. What I wanted to say was: what do I have in common with someone brought up in Pakistan? And, anyway, the minimum requirement for me, if I were to be fussy, was the ability to thread words together to form a sentence. Not a big ask, I didn't think. I didn't want to upset her further though, so I said, 'He didn't say a word to me. Anyway, I'm still married, Nana.'

I didn't want to hurt Nana's feelings. I knew she meant well. She and her mother, and her mother before her, all had arranged marriages. They were born and brought up in India and Pakistan and that was the way things were done. Nana had never even set eyes on her husband before their wedding day. She told me she was so keen to get a glimpse of her fiancé that she climbed on to an upside-down bucket in the bathroom and peered out of a small window, catching only the back of his head as he left. I, on the other hand, considered myself to be a modern, mixed-race British woman and there was no need for that archaic custom any more. In my opinion, arranged marriage was an outdated practice that should have been abolished aeons ago, as having no relevance in today's world. I knew it was different to 'forced' marriage, which was simply criminal and sacrilegious, but I also knew the two were often confused. And that was a problem in itself.

But there was a snag to all this judgement, a little voice in my head said. I had met Mr Right myself, the 'right' way, the way my upbringing considered normal, acceptable, and things should have been wonderful. The truth was, Mr Right had ended up being anything but.

Nana started to lecture me on the fact that husbands were not for conversation. That was not their purpose and there were many other people to satisfy that particular need (friends, relatives), as if any of this would alter my position on Midriff Man an iota. I changed the subject, bringing up the plans for the afternoon. This was a trick I'd relied on over the years; Nana, like a kitten, was easily distracted. She rushed off to get herself ready for our holy visit.

It was finally time to leave for the Data Darbar, the Wishing Place. We were going to spend the whole evening there in meditative prayer. As we stood to leave, the front door opened slowly and shadowed in a diffuse halo of light stood the holy man. Time slowed. He stepped in with Gandalf-like grace, stick in hand, and there behind him materialised the young man with the uncooked eyes, turquoise, gold, lapis lazuli. And those eyes, they were looking right at me.

# 12

# Ethereal Chilli Chutney (*page 40*)

For heavenly calm, take:

10 cloves garlic
6 green chillies
1 generous tbsp sea salt
butter, melted and warm (an essential accompaniment)
freshly made flatbread

The *taste*: unlike garlic, chilli or salt but something which is
neither one nor the other but so much more. It places fire on
the tongue, in the nose, in the eyes, and then leaves you
courageous.
The *artistry*: the juxtaposition of extremes where calm
results from fiery flavour.
The *purpose*: to calm and uplift and imbue fearlessness.

I'M NOT GOING TO SAY IT WAS ANNOYING TO HAVE A holy man turn up to take you personally to a holy shrine of a saint venerated by people all over the world, except that it was, a little at least. It had taken hours for me to prepare my petition to God (in writing, indexed and highlighted) in readiness for this visit to the Wishing Place and I didn't want the distraction of Mr Gorgeous Eyes, who, it seemed, accompanied Holy Man everywhere. As I had suspected, he was the son of Holy Man, a respected *Pir* who went by the name Abdal Basir.

I had formed the habit since being in Lahore of garnering information about plans and changes to plans by endeavouring to understand Nana's speedy exchanges in Urdu. Trouble was, with my Urdu skills, or lack of them, at any time I only managed to capture about 40% of what was being said, and even that took a lot of focus.

I was concentrating as Nana entered into animated conversation with Abdal Basir, so I didn't notice an arm being held forth to my right.

'Hi,' said the hovering hand. 'You must be Audrey.'

I swung round, my eavesdropping interrupted. 'Call me Addy,' I said. I took Mr Gorgeous Eyes' hand and shook it in a businesslike fashion.

'My father told me you're visiting from London.' He made his hand into a flying aeroplane as he said this and smiled. And then he said, 'I'm Huck.'

'Oh,' I said, 'as in Huckleberry Finn?'

'No, no. As in Abdal Haq. It's the truth.' He nodded, a jet curl falling onto his forehead.

'I didn't think it wasn't true.'

'No. My name, *Haq*, means the *truth*.'

This was not going well.

Haq observed me for a moment as if in deep thought, and then led me over to the sofa, his hand hovering at my lower back.

'Haq probably seems like a strange name to you. See, people here name their children carefully because they believe that the name you give someone can influence their personality. The word *Abdal* means *servant of*, and it's commonly coupled with one of the ninety-nine names of God.' He sat back on the sofa, his arms and legs in a spread. 'Have you heard of the ninety-nine names which describe the attributes of God?'

I had. Nana had taught me that God is beyond the reach of human imagination. I always liked this idea, because we are talking about the creator of the universe, and frankly I had difficulty truly grasping the magnitude of an ocean, let alone the earth, the sun, the solar system and so on. Nana said we know certain attributes of God through his 'beautiful names'. Names, she explained, like *Al Wadood* – the most loving – and *Al Baqi* – the one who has always existed without beginning or end, who is beyond the realm of time.

'Haq means the the truth, which is also a name of God. So, Abdal Haq translates as "the servant of the truth". And Abdal Basir, my father's name, translates as "the servant of the all-seeing", another of the ninety-nine names of God.' He went on to say that Abdal Basir wasn't his father's birth name, but it was given to him by his father's followers because, as a religious scholar, he was one of those rare few gifted with sight beyond this earthly, temporal realm. He was a seer.

'I see,' I replied, wishing I'd thought of another way of saying I understood.

I quizzed Haq about how his father and Nana knew each other and he told me that Nana and Holy Man came from families who had been friends going back generations. They had played together in the streets as children.

'And you?' I asked. 'Are you a religious scholar too?'

'No,' Haq said, 'I'm an IT consultant at IBM.'

Lahore and its people never stopped surprising me. Haq smiled. A big, giving smile, his eyes piercing, ethereal. In that moment, it seemed to me that time warped, so although it could only have been for a beat or two, the smile felt endless. Embarrassingly so. I became self-conscious, unsure where to place my eyes. Great beauty does that, affects you even if you don't want it to. After a moment, I smiled back, but averted my eyes, finding them focusing on the coffee table, the same one on which Midriff Man had maintained his unrelenting focus, and the thought made me look abruptly back at Haq. I appraised him as I turned to him, his angular figure, extremely slender form, his rich coffee-coloured skin, dark soft curls, all of this framing *those* eyes. I'd seen many beautiful eyes in my time – rich deep dark ones, pale icy ones, fresh foresty ones – but, in the flesh, I had never seen anything like those eyes before.

We headed out to the main road and Haq hailed a boldly coloured rickshaw that looked as if it'd been glued together as part of a school project. I challenged my fears and got in as he hailed another. The ride was bumpy and required fearlessness of a degree I had never needed access to before, the driver weaving through traffic and pedestrians missing each one by millimetres, if that. And all this in a motorised tricycle with a fabric roof and no doors. And of course, no seatbelts. I held a bar with one hand and my heart, to steady it, with the other. Jen held on to me. Nana sat cross-legged, serenely leaning back as if she were on a park bench, while Uncle Musa travelled up front with the driver. Haq and Holy Man in the other rickshaw dodged and darted between traffic in front of ours. Busy streets swept before my eyes: people, donkey carts, vehicles of all shapes and sizes, men in long shalwar kameez, men in suits and ties, women shrouded in lengthy scarfs, women in leggings with their cotton dresses sticking to their damp skins, and those in black burkhas covered from head to toe with only kohl-lined eyes visible. The only lengthy pause was for an ox-cart with a giant satellite dish in the rear to turn. The sight was striking: a weather-beaten, charcoal-skinned man wearing a turban and rags, tapping his ox with a cane to move this state-of-the-art, NASA-style technology to some other location.

When we arrived, I was struck with a sense of awe, in part for having survived such a perilous journey, but also from what I beheld. We were dropped at a street leading to the Data Darbar which was pulsating with festive energy. To our left were endless lines of food preparation stalls, where huge amounts of food were being cooked in containers Haq told me were called *deags* but could best be described as cauldrons. They were huge, round-bellied, and held enough to feed a multitude. It was a form of charitable offering to the poor. People would buy food in *deags* – lots – whether chicken, lamb or lentil, and this would be donated to feed the poor who attended the shrine and mosque. To our right was a stretch of rainbow-coloured stalls selling cut flowers, rose petals, bouquets and garlands. These were purchased to adorn the site and as gifts for visitors. Crowds flowed through the narrow street, splitting into rivulets here and there. People had come from all over the country and the world to worship God here and often to wish for specific things.

A large green dome strung with lights glowed above us. We gathered in a cluster at the mosque and then split apart, men to one side, women to the other. With the background hum of activity and movement, I wasn't sure how I was going to concentrate on prayers, but I had to try.

I had prayed before, with Nana at home mostly, and with Mum at church on Sundays, so I knew the format, but it was only standing here that I realised I hadn't ever *really* prayed. My prayers had, to date, been perfunctory, the ticking of boxes, following the lead of others. It's perplexing that as someone whose life had been surrounded by God, it was only now that I began to understand something about prayer and supplication.

The format of the prayer was as follows. The first and most important step was to state your intention – what it is you are about to do – which I did. Then, exactly as Nana had taught me, I stood and raised my hands so they were level with my ears, chanting 'God is greater', *Allah-hu akbar*, then I pushed the world away by a downward sweep of arms so I would not now, theoretically at least, permit any worldly distractions. I performed the ritual steps, bowing and kneeling and prostrating, while citing the set prayers I had learned. When the prayer was complete, I rose from my prostration, my forehead cold from the stone floor. At home, with Nana, I would cup my hands and raise them up to petition the Lord and then I would press my cupped palms together as Mum had taught me to do when supplicating at church. Here, however, none of that felt right. Here, I fell back down in prostration, forehead to the ground, and stayed there a while. I liked it. This way, a little dark vestibule was created by the enclosure formed of my forehead in contact with the ground and my arms about my head, either side blocking the light. A private, peaceful pocket. There, in the serenity of this space, I started, for the first time in my life, a conversation with God. And I was overcome with a sense that God heard and saw me, even though I could not see him.

*Dear God. I know I've not spoken to you before, even though, Lord knows, you've given me ample opportunity. I apologise. But Nana says you are entirely forgiving and that you'll forgive sins the size*

159

of the earth if we ask. I'm pretty sure anything I've done wrong isn't that big, but I start by asking your forgiveness for anything I've done wrong, knowingly or unknowingly. And thank you. Nana says gratitude is the most important thing, and even though what I am about to say may suggest I am not grateful, please don't take it that way. I am grateful for all the blessings in my life. My Nana, my Mum, my love of food, Jen, that we are all healthy and safe, and I'm not forgetting the seas, the skies, the universe and so on. I have a number of requests of you, God. To be clear, given this is an auspicious place and occasion, I have written down my petitions. I am sorry that the list is long and detailed and includes items that I shouldn't really bother you with, but Nana says the more I ask of you the better. Asking you, and you alone, for the biggest and smallest things being itself a mark of faith. So, I'll leave that with you. (I tapped my petition notebook inside my pocket.) Anyway, the biggest reason I'm here. I have a problem. My husband left me, and my terrible fate has made me miserable. Questions torment me day and night. Not knowing why hurts. Not knowing who, or even if there's another woman, is killing me. Please help me. What I have come to ask for is very specific. I want Gabe back. And I ask that you make him want me again. And please, please, could I find myself *pregnant, naturally, without the need for any medical intervention?*

I started to cry and plead, lamenting on and on until I was spent. When I rose, it was as if I had entered a great bubble of calm, engulfed with a sense of peace. A feeling that everything was going to be fine. That it always was, and always will be, just fine. The milling about of the crowds around me, unsettling as it was before, now became as comforting as the sound of a mountain stream. I'd heard it said that collective meditative thoughts and prayers send calming waves high into the air and that when they descend, they fall upon anyone who may by chance be in the vicinity, imbuing that calmness on them. I wondered now if this might be true.

Next, I reached into my pocket to retrieve my petition notebook, containing my detailed litany of requests to God which I had prepared back in London in readiness for this visit. It consisted of an enumerated list of my petitions in highlighted categories and set out in order of importance. There were also long tirades covering all my woes, regrets and disappointments and listing my wishes for the future. I wanted to be thorough, to be sure I didn't miss anything. I read from it in a whisper, line by line, handing over each worry and wish as I did, releasing it to the universe. Finally, when I was done, I put the notebook away and cast my eyes over the crowds. To my right, I saw Jen. She looked so sad, so absorbed in some meditative trance, that I thought she'd been crying, but I couldn't be sure. I made a mental note to ask her when we got home if she was okay. Through lines upon lines of heads, all still seated on the floor after prayers, I caught sight of Haq, his eyes closed, hands outstretched, palms up in supplication, lips moving slowly as he spoke invisible words.

After the prayers we found each other through the dispersing crowds and located a free corner of the vast courtyard area where we gathered into a circle on the floor. Uncle Musa brought over freshly cooked flatbreads wrapped in foil and a small pot of green paste called chilli chutney, a dish I had featured in my recipe book. I'd named it Ethereal Chilli Chutney for its particular ability to induce a near-spiritual state. The flatbreads or rotis were burning hot and dripping with melted butter. You tear a bit off and dip one corner ever so lightly (unless you are a braver person than me) into the paste. The taste is totally sensational. Although reminiscent of garlic bread, garlic bread is the infant child of the muscular Adonis that is chilli chutney.

As we ate, I asked Nana about the locked door at home behind which Aunty Gulu had said was the residence of a djinn. Nana nodded, took a great bite of roti, and when she'd finished, she spoke.

'Let me tell you that story,' she said. 'I will start from the beginning.' In a mix of English with Urdu dotted between (which I translated for Jen when I could), she told the tale.

When Nana was young, she was known for her beauty, she said. So much so that she would leave a wake of turned heads on the street (as I've said, Nana doesn't do modesty). She had recently married and was preparing dinner as she did each day, and afterwards she moved to chores in the bedroom. Part way through, she realised she had forgotten to bless the meal as she was preparing it. She had been brought up with the belief that blessing the meal was important because otherwise it might not nourish you. As she was returning to the kitchen, she became distracted by a sound in the garden. She heard birdsong she'd never heard before and it seemed to her that instead of singing in random, varied bursts, the way birds do, they were singing the same tremulous warble in unison like a bird choir. She unlocked the door, but as she stepped into the garden, the sound stopped. And, stranger still, there wasn't a bird to be seen anywhere. There was only the local black cat, staring up at her. Feeling sorry for the cat, who she felt must surely be thirsty, she coaxed it into her house for milk. She had virtually adopted this stray over the past few months.

Later, when it was clear that her husband, my Grandpa, would be home late that evening, she decided to take some mustard spinach to her father, my great-grandfather, who lived a short walk away. She packed a tiffin with the spinach and headed over to her father's home.

'This marks the beginning of a series of terrible and mysterious happenings,' Nana said. 'I saw things. Otherworldly things . . .' She pulled up her sleeve to reveal the goosebumps that had appeared on her arm.

And then, with a gentle shaking of her head, she stopped her story abruptly, saying it was getting late and was time to go. We stood to leave. The rest of the story would have to continue another time.

On the way home, Holy Man spoke to me at the back of the rickshaw with the help of Haq, who translated when the need arose. He had kind, soft eyes, and a gentle voice. I noticed he was wearing a small parcel of fabric on his wrist, tied on with string.

'What's that?' I asked.

'This is a *taweez*,' he said, 'for protection.' A *taweez*, I discovered, is a kind of amulet, often consisting of words from the Holy Book, copied out and then tightly wrapped in protective plastic. This package is then placed in a fabric wrapping so it can be worn. Such things, Holy Man told me, are to be kept on at all times.

'This one protects and directs the wearer. Others serve different purposes.'

'What kinds of purposes?'

'Anything you may want in your life, or anything that may be causing you upset or anxiety.' He caught my thoughts and after a pause said, 'Here take this.' He tied the *taweez* on my wrist. I was deeply grateful. It wasn't that I believed in such things, but I was always open to the possibility. How can we really know, I thought?

'But Addy,' Abdal Basir said, 'remember, God chooses. We must trust that everything that happens to us happens for the best. Trust that you are being directed and cared for, no matter how bad things may seem. When you truly trust and accept both the good and bad in life as gifts (even if you cannot see the good), then you will see wonders.'

I nodded obediently, even though I didn't understand.

Back at home, it was late evening when Uncle Musa came to me.

'How did you enjoy the Data Darbar?'

'Uncle, it was amazing.' He smiled, and rubbed his palm on the back of his neck, just as Dad used to.

'Data Ganj Baksh was an amazing man of God. A scholar. He would say the true people of God "have terrestrial bodies in celestial abodes".'

'I love the sound of that, Uncle,' I said.

'Did you make any wishes? Because they say supplications after prayers there are always answered.'

At this I produced my indexed and highlighted booklet of wishes and supplications. I felt close enough to Uncle Musa, given that he was Nana's son, to show him. He was a little dazzled.

'This is . . . impressive,' he said, paging through the endless list.

'I know. I didn't want to forget to ask for something.'

Uncle Musa pondered a while, looking between me and my book. 'You know, Addy, one of the most beautiful aspects of prayers for me is to simply place myself in the presence of God. Just be. It's a wonderful feeling, although it can take some work to get there.'

'Really. You don't petition for things?'

'Sometimes, if there is something pressing and it's helpful for me. But you know, I always think God knows.'

I dropped my head. 'There is something pressing for me, Uncle. About Gabe. I feel I've been deserted by him as if there was never a relationship in the first place. It's so callous – the worst kind of hurt.'

Uncle Musa's face was pinched, his eyes glassy as he slowly shook his head in acknowledgment. I could feel his love. That was something I'd learned; there was so much compassion in the people here. I hadn't intended to upset him, so I changed the subject.

'Uncle, there's no time like the present. Can I interview you now?'

'*Beta*, it's late,' he said.

'Oh please, Uncle. I wanted to know everything about your life here, and about Dad.'

'Another time,' he said as he left the room in a hurry.

In bed, nearly asleep, my voice breathy with exhaustion, I told Nana it had been a wonderful day. She grunted in semi-slumber. And then a thought came to me.

'Nana,' I said, 'why did you ask us to hand the children at the fruit stall our gift-money with our palms up?'

'Because,' Nana slurred, 'things are not as they appear.' She tucked her sheet under her chin. Yawned. 'You believe you are giving them a gift, but it is they that are bestowing a gift on you. God has given you an opportunity to receive a good deed. That is the true gift. Palm up is a reminder you are getting, not giving.'

I considered this. 'And the fruit, Nana. Why did you pick the bruised fruit from the fruit seller?' There was no reply. Nana was already whistling her way into a deep sleep.

As I lay in bed that night, those dark, spiralling thoughts didn't come. Instead I recalled the pocket of calm I had felt at the Data Darbar shrine. At that time, in that moment, I felt it again. Peace. Contentment. Calm. In this atmosphere of serenity, as I drifted off, I realised myself why Nana had taken the bruised fruit. It was an act of charity to that poor market trader.

That this was the calm before the proverbial storm, I could not have known. Nothing could have prepared me for what was about to hit.

# 13

# Stay-Steady Jelly Soup (*page 41*)

For resolve to rise within and strengthen you, take:

1 onion, finely sliced
3 garlic cloves, crushed
1 small piece ginger, roughly chopped
5-6 lamb's trotters
8cm/3in cinnamon stick
a pinch of cumin seeds
a few black peppercorns
1/2 tsp turmeric
1/2 tsp coriander powder
a dash of chilli
salt
a mug of yogurt
2-3 litres water, to boil

The *taste*: lush and rich and glutinous.
The *artistry*: the quality of uniqueness to move you outside
of your comfort zone.
The *purpose*: to inspire the love and warmth of an endless
hug that fills you with a sense of worthiness.

THE FOLLOWING DAY, NANA WAS AT IT AGAIN.

Arrangements had been made for Haq to take Jen and me to Urdu Bazaar, Lahore's largest book market, at some point during the day. I'd planned on buying a pestle and mortar at a place nearby where they painstakingly chiselled them by hand from stone and wood. However, I had prepared myself to wait until at least late afternoon for the outing because nothing happened in a timely or efficient manner in Lahore, something I was getting used to. Shortly after a phenomenal breakfast of poori, halva and chick peas – the halva sweet, the chick peas savoury, and the deep-fired poori bread chewy – I had to have a rest. As I made myself comfortable on a pink sofa, Nana and a woman with a son in tow arrived. At least, it could have been her son, but there was no way to be sure. There was no resemblance. This man, as a matter of fact, bore no resemblance to any member of the human race. He looked more like someone who'd left the world of the living a while back. And yet this seemed to be of no consequence to Nana, who launched into animated chat with his mother. Tea and biscuits appeared, as before. This time, I noticed Nana glancing over at me, her stern eye urging me to converse.

Although it was irrational, I couldn't help being a little afraid of him. Ghost Man seemed to have two modes, full-volume and mute, and he inspired a defensive instinct in me, most probably due to his intense, accusatory glaring during his full-volume mode. Then, when he looked away from me, his lids would lower as if he'd fallen asleep while still seated, entering his mute mode. To be fair to him, he did at least try to converse, or rather he spat and coughed his views at me.

'Do you work here in Lahore?' I asked.

'Yes,' he said at full volume. 'I am a senior lecturer at Soandso College. It is very hard to get in, you know. One of the best. This you should know.' He then went mute and turned away.

In answer to 'Do you live far from here?'

'Defence Housing Authority,' he said in a near shout. 'You probably don't know that either. It's the best area in Lahore. Best. Don't believe anyone who tells you something else.' He then went mute again.

I wished he'd taken an interest in the coffee table, like Midriff Man.

After the passage of a reasonable period of time (four minutes by the clock on the wall), I excused myself, breaking into a near run at the approach to the stairs, not stopping until I was in my room, door closed.

Nana came up after they'd left. 'Where did you go, *beta*?'

I gave her The Look.

'So you didn't like him either.'

'Nana, please. I'm not even divorced yet.'

'Pah, forget that *jahil*, ignoramus. He doesn't deserve you. *Kafir!*'

'Nana,' I said, starting to feel irritated but trying to calm myself, 'I understand you mean well, but really, this whole intro thing, it's not for me. And even it was for me, him! Please, Nana.' Thank goodness I'd had a good breakfast to help me cope.

Nana nodded as if in agreement, but I had seen this all my life. The Nod. Not to be mistaken for acquiescence of any variety. Nana was the most stubborn and wilful person I knew.

Shortly after, Nana, Jen and I were eating a mountain of fruit at the table as Uncle Musa chopped and peeled. Nana was continuing the story she'd started about the djinn at the Data Darbar shrine, Jen and I both listening eagerly, desperate to hear what Nana had seen that day.

Nana had headed over to her father's home, passing children playing tag and street merchants urging her to buy prayer beads and sweets. Her father, my great-grandfather, was a *Pir*. A saintly man of great knowledge and spirituality possessing a connection with God rarely observed these days. He came from a lineage of very religious people who claim a bloodline to the prophet Muhammad himself: a lineage called *Sayyid*.

When Nana entered his house, he was in deep meditative prayer, seated on the floor upon a prayer mat in the traditional way, intermittently lowering his forehead so it made contact with the ground and reciting *Subhan Allah*, meaning 'glory be to God', on his prayer beads.

Nana sat behind him on a low bed. (As she spoke, she edged forward, her eyes widening. Jen and I stopped chewing; Uncle Musa's knife was held suspended in midair.) As she was waiting, a tiny figure appeared out of nowhere, seated in the far corner of the room. Nana leapt over to her father, about to scream, but was stopped by her father's outstretched arm. This thing resembled a human but was much smaller. There, in the corner of the room, he started beating raw cotton to form an ever-growing ball of flax. My great-grandfather continued to pray, unfazed, my Nana hiding behind him. He knew it was a distraction, sent to tempt him from his prayers and supplications. The little person continued to work; the cloud of cotton wool continued to grow. Eventually it grew so big it filled the corner of the room. My great-grandfather didn't pause or break his prayers, absorbed in his devotional meditation. After a while the cotton wool filled the entire room and the little man stood before them and lit a match, setting the cotton alight. There was a great explosive flash, blinding beautiful light, and the cotton went up in flames. My Nana screamed, but all the while, my great-grandfather was unflinchingly absorbed in his prayers.

And then the hobbit was gone, along with the flames. Nothing was even scorched.

It was after this, as my great-grandfather comforted my Nana, that *they* appeared; Nana whispered the word *they*.

'Who?' Jen asked.

The djinn folk. It started as a mist, barely there. You might have thought, at first, you had something in your eye. Then, like a gathering fog, slowly they took form, these amorphous, translucent beings. Their appearance was much like you might imagine a ghost, only they were very tall and had a wavy peak flaming in a roughly triangular shape above their heads, swaying slowly. Over the space of about a minute, they became visible as a crowd of bodies in the room, their feet floating the smallest distance above the ground. The one who spoke on their behalf introduced himself as John, which led to Nana being convinced for ever after that John was a Pakistani name, perhaps from the Kalash people of the North.

'You have passed the test of faith. We are in search of someone to teach us the Holy Book, someone of true faith, who does not waver in the face of danger. And we choose you.'

My great-grandfather considered this, all the while not ceasing his repetition of the praise *Subhan Allah*. 'And what will I get in return?'

'What do you want from us?' they asked.

Nana said she came to understand the importance of bargaining with the djinn for protection, because experts on these gaseous creatures will tell you they are tricksy beings.

'Teach me something of your ways,' he said.

They agreed. 'What would you like to know?' John said.

My great-grandfather looked to my Nana, and without thinking, given her love of cookery, she asked about what they ate.

'We eat a great many things, but our favourite is a dish made from bone.'

There was a whisper amongst the djinn.

Then one from amongst them spoke. 'We can bring you the dish to try if you like.'

It was no surprise to Nana to hear that bone was the main ingredient of the dish, for it was a commonly held belief amongst the people of Pakistan that djinn ate bones. And this was not allegory or fantasy; it was a simple fact, in the way one may say butterflies like nectar. This was why, Nana said, whenever a meal included bones, she would chant precautionary prayers so as not to attract these beings to our home and, especially, to ward away the evil ones. She didn't know how the djinn folk would prepare a meal with such an ingredient, though.

'I would like to see it made for myself,' Nana's father said. 'Bring the ingredients and my daughter will make it with your people, in my kitchen.'

And this, Nana said, was how my great-grandfather became a teacher to the djinn. And how it came to pass that Nana herself cooked with the spirit people, learning from them an age-old recipe made of bone.

Nana had never told me this story from her younger days before, but in London, she had taught me how to make the dish. It is glorious. It was noted in my Ms Mayford recipe book on page 41. I now decided I would name this dish, a dish I now knew to be from the world of the djinn, Stay-Steady Jelly Soup, or Gloup for short, as it has a glutinous consistency. It is an astonishing, otherworldly dish, full of depth and character and warmth. A dish so luscious and flavoursome,

I can promise that you have never tasted anything like it in your life. It has the quality of soup, and is eaten with nan bread, slathered with butter, which is dipped into the sauce. Some people may be reluctant to try this dish, it being so different, so outside of their comfort zone. I marvelled at the thought that had my ancestors not been gifted with this encounter we would not have this dish to savour.

After the deal was struck between the djinn folk and Nana's father that he would teach the djinn how to read the Holy Book, and that in return they would teach Nana their favourite dish, Nana rose to leave and the djinn said their farewells. There is no such thing as a handshake between man and djinn, although they do have a greeting and farewell gesture, which resembles a high five, the contact of palms remaining for some three seconds.

But there was more.

What nobody knew was that when Nana left my great-grandfather's house to return to her home, she did not leave alone. There was one fewer in the group of djinn that remained with my great-grandfather, because one had secretly left with my Nana and followed her. And when she entered her home that afternoon, feeling unbearably hot from his presence, even though the sun was low in the sky, he slipped in through the door behind her, as close and as unseen as her own shadow.

'Why did he follow you home?' Jen said.

Just then, a knock on the door announced the arrival of Haq to take us to Urdu Bazaar. Jen complained about an upset stomach, due to all the fruit we had eaten while listening to Nana's story, and said she couldn't join us.

What a relief it was to see a normal human man. No trollish traits or ghoulish skull formations in sight.

# 14

# Nothing is Impossible Pink Tea
### (*page 45*)

For eyes to go from blind to seeing, hearts to shift and possibilities to open up, take:

Kashmiri tea leaves, 1 tsp per cup
4-6 cups boiling milk and water
1/2 tsp salt
1/2 tsp baking soda
1 star anise
1 cinnamon stick

The *taste:* like a kiss upon the lips.
The *artistry:* transformation within yourself, by making the familiar unfamiliar.
The *purpose:* to open the heart, so you see that to which you may otherwise have been blind.

THE ROUTE THROUGH LAHORE IN TRAFFIC WAS AS traumatic as ever, with everyone in a desperate hurry to get somewhere. It meant overcrowding, lawlessness and fearlessness, all visible in glorious high definition. The end result was logjam; no one got anywhere fast. I quickly discovered horn honking was a purposeless pastime in which everyone partook. Whole families piled on to a single motorbike, while on the same stretch of road were top-end cars, bicycles, donkey carts, rickshaws, people on foot walking centrally, as if roads were a pedestrian facility, and those massive, ornately decorated trucks moving like dinosaurs through a stream. Our rickshaw driver in small stretches reached motorway speeds, dodging and swerving without a care. We arrived, nerves shattered, but intact. And it was worth it.

The area near Urdu Bazaar where pestle and mortars

were made could be heard at a distance. The tap-a-tap sounds of an endless crowd of workers who sat on the floor, either in the open or under makeshift canopies, rose as a magnificent rhythmic drumbeat. The options were as limitless as the different types of wood and stone used. There was black granite, smooth brown stone, white marble and endless woods, many with ornate carvings. Most were too big or heavy to carry back on a rickshaw, let alone a plane. Haq looked amused at my fascination for these curious implements. Eventually, I chose a design I'd never seen before, which consisted of a tall, narrow stone mortar and a long wooden pestle. The maker who demonstrated it showed how you had to stand to use it and explained that when you plunged the wooden pestle down, the contents could not escape, due to the height and narrow width of the mortar. I decided I'd work out how to get it on to a plane later.

We wandered around taking everything in, stopping at times for Haq to introduce someone. One was an elderly man with skin hanging from his forearms like beige fabric. He'd worked as a craftsman there every day for sixty years. He insisted I accept a gift of a miniature pestle and mortar and refused payment. Then there were kids everywhere, barely ten years old at a guess, and yet so skilled with a chisel, when elsewhere in the world they'd be playing with Lego blocks or watching superhero movies on television rather than selling their wares. The whole experience felt as if I had entered a different universe. The generosity and warmth of these hard-working, desperately poor people was palpable, and it shifted something in me.

We'd been walking a while now. I'd noticed before how so much of Lahore carried the scent of wood smoke, reminiscent of an autumnal Guy Fawkes evening in London. As I breathed in deep, enjoying the smell, I caught the scent of Haq and breathed in some more. It was a warm, alluring man-scent, the sort that draws you in, mixed with threads of detergent, and something dark and rich. I recognised it as Oud, a scent popular in the subcontinent and Middle East and quite unlike any smell in the Western world, except that Jen, being a beauty products aficionado, had informed me it was now being trickled into certain top-end perfume brands.

'You must be tired, Addy,' Haq said.

'No, I'm okay. Just overwhelmed, is all.'

Haq smiled that smile, the one that held nothing back. 'Come, let's sit down here for a bit.' He steered me towards plastic garden chairs beside a donkey cart, upon which tea was being served from a giant steel vat. He sat back in the chair and stretched. 'It's wonderful here, isn't it?' he said.

'It's special for sure. Thanks for bringing me,' I said, one hand upon my newly purchased pestle and mortar.

'Your family are very important to us. They're lovely people,' he said.

'I can't wait to find out more about them, especially about what my father was like,' I said. 'I wish I could have known him better.'

I noticed a subtle frown on Haq's brow. 'It must be hard, with you living so far away,' he said. I nodded sleepily, watching the *chai-wala* stir the boiling tea, lifting it in his giant ladle and then releasing it in a great stream back into the vat. It took a moment before I noticed that the colour of the tea was baby pink.

'Kashmiri chai,' Haq said noticing me looking puzzled. 'It's a speciality made from green tea leaves, milk and baking soda, and they prepare it in a samovar, that decorated metallic urn you see there. It's so delicious, just wait and see.' I was certain this would soon be added to my Ms Mayford recipe book.

'You know I'm going to interview my family here in Lahore, actually record my conversations?' I wasn't sure why I was telling Haq this.

'That's a great idea. Why don't you practise on me?'

I laughed. 'Perhaps,' I said, adding that I thought Aunty Gulu was going to be a very interesting subject.

'She's never been "all there", for sure. I could tell you some crazy stories about her,' he said. And then after a pause, 'So what brought you here?'

I pulled in a breath, the reasons racing about in my

mind. 'Well, because of Nana. She virtually forced me. And . . . Gabe,' I braved, feeling a pinch at having voiced his name.

'Gabe?'

'Yes. He's my husband, or rather was until he walked out on me, and . . .' And what? I thought. There was no way for me to complete the sentence.

Haq became still, a pained expression on his face. 'That's terrible.' He sat motionless, seemingly deep in thought, observing me.

I didn't know where to look and so I nodded and cast my eyes about the place.

'I can't imagine anyone doing that to you,' he said, his eyes intense, a severe, unreadable expression on his face.

'Nor can I,' I said, laughing to break the tension, kill my rising tears. 'It's good for me, though, you know . . . to get away from it all. And this definitely qualifies as getting away. Lahore is a parallel universe.'

Haq laughed too.

'I'd hate to shatter your illusions, but there are shopping malls here, and yes, even a McDonald's.'

I looked into his eyes, holding my breath at the sight. They were so captivating.

'And now? How do you feel about things now?'

I cast my eyes down, as if the answer lay somewhere around my feet. Devastated, destroyed, forever damaged didn't make for great conversation. 'Wait a minute. Am I not meant to be interviewing you?' I said, relieved at my opportunity to escape his questions.

'I'm all yours,' he said, throwing himself back in his chair. 'Where do you want to start?'

I pondered for a moment and then reached over, fist tight, as if I had a microphone in my hand. 'So, Haq, "the Truth",' I said with exaggerated confidence. 'Tell me about yourself.' I was surprised at the genuine depth of my curiosity. 'Do you have a girlfriend, a fiancée?'

He pulled in a slow, deep breath, his smile fading. 'Well, I am engaged,' he said, and then, as his name was called, 'Hold on.'

I waited as he went to collect our Kashmiri chai. He returned with two plastic cups and a sticky orange spiral in a large paper cupcake holder.

'*Jalebi*,' he announced. 'This stuff is fantastic; you must try it. But it's very sticky, so here . . .' He broke off a piece and raised it to my mouth. I held his wrist to steady and catch the dripping syrup, then sank my teeth into it. And oh! It was both crispy and chewy, soft and hard, sweet with an undertone of savoury lentil. In short, magnificent.

'Oh, I have to get the recipe for this. It's *amazing*.'

'Another one for your book?' Haq said. He must have seen the puzzled look on my face and so added, 'Your Nana told me you've been putting a recipe book together for years.' I wasn't sure how I felt about Nana sharing such things.

'Look,' Haq said, pointing subtly behind me, 'you can tell people here enjoy *jalebi*.' Behind me was a rotund man with a whole plate of *jalebi*, piled high.

'This is all amazing, Haq,' I said, sipping the sweet, salty, creamy pink tea which was an entirely new sensation for me. To describe it would be like describing honey to someone who's never tasted it. Viscous sugar doesn't even come close.

'This is nothing. There is so much more I want to show you,' he said, leaning in and studying me as he spoke. Something tightened in the pit of my stomach. Pleasant and uncomfortable at the same time. 'Why have you not visited Lahore before?' he asked.

'Not a chance. I'm interviewing you, remember.'

He raised his arms in submission. 'So?' I continued, moving the subject away from me and hoping the effect he was having on me wasn't visible, 'As you were saying, you're engaged.'

Haq downed the rest of his tea, taking big gulps, and raised his arm to the seller for another. 'Yes, yes, I am,' he said, sounding almost apologetic. 'And she's beautiful. Farah and I have exchanged gifts and I've given her the customary gold jewellery sets, the way you do here . . . but . . .' I could see he was having difficulty with this, 'she's making more and more demands. Things she wants, where and how she wants to live. There's this whole checklist thing going on. And I have to confess, I feel uncomfortable, invisible almost. Like I'm just another item on her list.' He rubbed his temples. 'So I told my mother I wasn't sure whether I wanted this.' He pulled in a breath. 'And she's furious.'

'And your father? How does he feel?'

'Dad understands my dilemma. But I don't know . . . it's a tricky situation. Our *nikah*, that's the marriage registry, is very soon. We've decided it'll just be a small family thing, since the wedding celebrations themselves are so big. I've taken time off work to help with the arrangements.' He looked directly at me. 'You'll meet her tonight at the restaurant, and I'll definitely bring her over to Nana's place sometime.' And then, sitting forward in his chair, 'My turn now.'

'But I haven't finished!'

'Too bad. You'll have to be patient, it's only fair,' he said. 'You tell me now. How do you feel about things with your husband?'

I paused. Mustering courage to find words, even though my throat was closing. 'I don't know really. It's still raw. You see, I . . . I think there's someone else. Another woman. And I feel so angry. As much for him not telling me why he left as for walking out. He's cut me off completely now, won't answer my calls or texts. This fury, this sadness and not knowing, it's eating me up.'

Haq nodded. His eyes were slim, his brow furrowed.

'But the funny thing is, now, so far away, I feel like the space between Gabe and me is helping me. I think there's still a chance for us. Sometimes I worry that I'd dreamed it all up in my head, the idea of this other woman.'

'Intuition can be the best guide.'

'Sometimes I have this near panic attack thinking I may have ruined everything, all by myself. And I keep questioning, what did I do wrong?' I pulled in a deep breath, my chest tightening with these corrosive memories.

'Why are you blaming yourself, Addy? Don't.' Haq shunted his chair closer to me. 'He's the one that walked away, remember.' He tipped his head closer, his eyes boring into mine, and gently, almost in a whisper, said, 'You don't deserve this. So don't torture yourself.'

The man with the *jalebis* rose to leave and the scraping of his chair against the earth broke Haq's focus. I noticed I'd been holding my breath, and released the trapped air.

'I think you're right, Haq,' I said. 'But see, self-torture; that's my thing. I've got it nailed.'

He studied my face for a long while, as if weighing up whether to say something. 'You know my father is a religious scholar, and there's this great saying he often quotes. It goes something like, we should aim to be people who do not fear or grieve. Fear being worry about the future, and grief being regret about the past.'

'So we should stay in the present, the now?'

'Yes. And whenever people come to him with stories of the terrible things they've been through, he always tells them to accept the bad in life in the same way we do the good things that happen to us. It's all from God, the good and the bad. It all happens for a reason.'

'But why couldn't Gabe just tell me straight why he was leaving? That's what hurts, and now he's cut me off completely. No contact at all, no matter how much I've reached out to him. That's the source of my suffering. I think that's what's broken me,' I said, a momentary memory of Dad's abandonment before he died entering my mind.

Haq reached over to me. Hesitated, then lightly touched my hand. 'Broken things mend, Addy. Sometimes they end up stronger, better than before,' he said, and then, pulling away, added, 'People are strange.'

We both took a few sips of tea.

'And now Nana's trying to set me up with a "suitable" new man,' I said.

Haq laughed. 'That wouldn't surprise me. It's a national pastime here. A default setting in the Pakistani mindset. Any single person is always introduced to random suitors. Being single and of marriageable age is a status they don't recognise. You shouldn't be offended; they mean well.'

'I know,' I said, resigned. 'But you should see these guys! And anyway, I don't get this arranged marriage thing. How can anyone marry someone they don't know, haven't spent any time with? It's an insane notion . . .' I quickly added, 'in my view,' given there was every likelihood Haq's marriage was being arranged.

'I can see how you may think that, Addy. But it's more of an introduction really, and . . .' He paused, then continued, 'I mean, did you ever really know Gabe, given . . .'

He didn't complete the sentence. I looked away, then changing the subject, I said, 'Anyway, I think your father's right. Perhaps we should just accept things the way they really are, however bad.'

'It's called *Rida*, this idea,' Haq said. 'It's part of the philosophy my father teaches to help us cope with challenges in life. It means the serene acceptance of everything past and future that happens to you. To accept it with calm resignation, or even cheerfully. There's this book he teaches called *Degrees of the Soul* by an Egyptian scholar who wrote a series of 'recipes' for acquiring such traits, the hope being you raise your character higher and higher so that one day you might become a "friend of God", the way the chosen ones were. It is said that it's not enough for these saints to "know" these great truths; they want to "taste" them.'

Haq's words went largely over my head, except the words 'taste' and 'recipe'.

'Perhaps he can teach me,' I said. 'See, I just love recipes. And I've always wished someone would write up a recipe on how to get life right. How wonderful that would be.'

Haq nodded, a little surprised at my enthusiasm. 'There's this story that a saint was said to have told. A dervish fell into a river. A man spotted him and shouted, "Shall I bring someone to rescue you?" The dervish said, "No." The man said, "Do you wish to die?" The dervish said, "No." The man asked, "What do you wish?" To which the dervish replied, "I wish what God wishes. I have nothing to do with wishing."'

We both laughed.

'Addy, next question. What's the craziest thing you've done?'

'Wait, it's my turn,' I said. 'And I'm the one who's meant to be practising my interviewing technique, remember?'

'You next then. Promise.'

I thought for a while. 'Well, there was this time I was hauled before the headmaster for sniffing something. I was ordered to turn out my pockets and so I had to show him the clove of garlic in my pocket, sliced in half, raw and still damp.'

'And you did this because . . .'

'I was young. I loved the smell of garlic.'

Haq laughed.

'I only sniffed it in private, like behind the bike sheds, but I got caught. Really confused the headmaster.'

Haq was now laughing more than was called for. 'I think I'd better surrender. Can't beat that.'

'No way. It's your turn. What's the craziest thing *you've* done?'

Haq recovered himself, his face became calm. He thought for a brief while before speaking. 'Agreeing to marry someone I'm not sure about to please my mother.'

I looked away. Neither of us was laughing now. We sat for a while, occasionally glancing at each other as we sipped endless cups of pink tea, surrounded by the rhythmic beating of stone being chiselled. After a short while an idea came to me.

'Haq,' I said, 'let me cook for you.'

'Why?'

'Because I have the perfect recipe and I think you need it.' I paused for a moment, wondering how honest to be with him. 'It'll help you make up your mind about your engagement. See, I also hold certain beliefs, like your dad. I believe there are things that you wouldn't suspect can help you cope with life, that could even *change* your life. Certain recipes, certain ingredients, when combined in a particular way, have power.' I could hardly believe I was telling Haq, was sure he'd think me completely crazy. Despite this, I carried on. 'And there's this dish that could help you make up your mind about whether you should marry your fiancée.' I pulled in a deep breath, my eyes racing about his face for signs of his reaction.

He thought for a few beats. Then, nodding serenely, said, 'How could I refuse an offer like that?'

'Good,' I said. 'It's settled then.'

As we smiled at each other, an old, toothless woman in clean white clothing approached, reaching out her hand for baksheesh. She spoke a dialect neither Haq nor I could understand. Haq said it was probably Farsi. She was trying to communicate something, pointing between her scarf and then her neck, but it was no use. There was no way to bridge the language gap. And then she said, '*Bismillah*.' I repeated it. Everyone knew that word; it meant 'in the name of God'. Next, catching hold of this idea, she recited the first line of the Lord's prayer of the Muslims, *Surah Al-Fatiha*, the Opening. A prayer everyone knows. I recited the second line. She recited the third and then in unison we recited the rest. She embraced me and then turned to leave. I called her back. 'Baksheesh,' I said, holding out my hand. The notes were folded in my palm. I flipped it 180 degrees, palm up, and gave the money to her.

Haq looked at his watch. 'We'd better get going. Aren't we going to your family's favourite restaurant for dinner this evening? We don't want to be late.'

'You're right.' I said, knowing there was no such thing as 'being late' here in Lahore.

Haq hailed a rickshaw, unaware he'd selected a kamikaze driver, the craziest so far. He steadied me in the back, his arm around my waist as we were whipped from side to side. I took refuge in his steady chest. He called out over the noise, as I buried myself in him, 'Actually, change of plan. I'm taking you to the Palace of Mirrors, Addy, the Sheesh Mahal, one of my favourite places in Lahore. A palace from the Mughal era, embedded with a thousand mosaic mirrors.'

'Oh my God. My Dad told me about it when I was a child,' I said, memories of my Dad filling my mind.

'It's a bit broken,' I say, as Haq walks me around the palace.

'Well, it is a ruin.'

'I thought when you said palace, it would be like Buckingham or Windsor.'

Haq sighs. 'You're a tough girl to please.'

We walk under scalloped arches, on tiles in ever-repeating hexagons. Haq revels in my joy as I step through the courtyard, touching the engraved walls. Flowers raised to life, forever in red stone. Everywhere we look, a thousand broken images look back, the broken parts together feeling whole. Colour rising to more colour, shapes to more shapes, endlessly spiralling. I spin under hexagonal blossoms caught within the marble walls, feel the magic of the place, my mind filling with stories of the Arabian Nights that Nana used to tell. Scheherazade and her tales that circled like the rotating patterns on the walls.

'You're dancing like Anarkali, or at least the actress who played her,' Haq says.

I smile, steading my dizziness against a wall, and watch him examine a mosaic.

He turns; his eyes meet mine and I quickly look away. 'Do you know the story, Addy? The prince who fell in love with a courtesan.'

I cannot respond. Haq is standing in a pool of shattered light cast from a million mirrored shards.

'The story goes that she was chased out of town by the prince's father, the Mughal emperor, after he learned of their love. The emperor then had her buried alive in the walls.'

'Romantic,' I say, a note of sarcasm in my tone. 'I wonder why stories of love so often end in murder?' My hand strokes the wall, the stone cool beneath my fingertips as I speak.

'The marketplace, one of the largest in Lahore, now bears her name,' Haq continues. 'And there's this mausoleum nearby which celebrates their love.'

'I'm sure my father told me that story. When I was really young. Between Anarkali and Scheherazade, you'd think all men want to do is hurt or murder women. Love. It's a war zone,' I say. I tip my head in resignation. 'I feel like Anarkali.'

Haq looks amused. 'You're not being sentenced to death,' he says, 'I hope.'

I give him a look. 'There are many ways to die . . .' I say, sighing melodramatically as I speak.

Haq steps forward, one step, then another, his eyes unwaveringly on mine. 'I'm guessing you haven't heard the story of Layla and Majnun then?'

I cannot respond. I allow myself to look at his eyes, drink them in as he moves to me, so close that I can feel his warmth, his breath.

'Not all men are like that,' he whispers, his finger moving in an arc upon my cheek.

There is fire in my skin. I have the sensation I'm falling. My breath deepens as his finger draws feather-like across my skin. He sweeps a strand of hair and tucks it in behind my ear, where it immediately falls back out again. I smile. I am magnetised, am willing him to reach for me again. But then I think of Gabe and drop my head.

He moves away, brow rippling. There's something in his eyes. Guilt, perhaps? I don't know. I cast my own eyes about as if I'm looking at the walls.

But all I really see is him.

# 15

# Calm-Making Cauliflower
## (*page 47*)

For calmness which brings clarity and decisiveness, take:

1 cauliflower, sliced

10-12 small chunks of lamb, diced or on the bone

1 onion, sliced

5 garlic cloves, minced

2 tsp garam masala

1 tsp chilli powder

2/3 tomatoes

a knob of butter to melt on the top

The taste: deep, vegetal and soothing, with a meaty warm base. Exceptional and unique.

The artistry: the power to transform the underrated, near despised (cauliflower) and show that everything has capacity for majesty.

The purpose: to still the mind, quiet the chatter, so when you have an important choice to make, you are calmed to a near meditative state, enabling confusion to clear.

LATER THAT EVENING, SEVERAL FAMILY MEMBERS AND friends, including Holy Man and Haq, were meeting at a *taka tak* restaurant, the name being onomatopoeic, from the tapping sound of meat being chopped rhythmically as it is cooked on giant circular hotplates. I remember as a child how Dad had told me that the *taka tak* restaurants were his favourite, so it felt special that we were going to be eating at one. Haq had said he would bring his fiancée Farah this evening too. I'd heard Nana whisper she was said to be an extraordinary beauty and I found myself a little too eager to see if the rumours were true.

On the way there in the taxi, my thoughts rested on Haq. Rolling memories laced with guilt about the way he'd looked at me and the butterfly touch of his fingertips on my face. It was not as if I actually had anything to be guilty about, but being Catholic, Muslim and married, a reason wasn't necessary.

After the visit to the Sheesh Mahal, Haq had helped me carry the pestle and mortar from the rickshaw to the house. I told him I'd decided I wanted to buy another. A smaller stone one for grinding whole dried spices.

'We should probably get this one home first, don't you think?' he'd said. And then, 'I'm starting to wonder if London's a little primitive.'

'What do you mean?'

'Don't you have electricity, like for blenders, food processors?'

I laughed. 'We do. It's just I have an affinity for hand-crafted things because their makers leave behind a part of themselves, at least that's what I believe.' I ran my hands over the smooth, cool stone of the mortar, feeling the undulations of imperfect human effort. 'See,' I said, 'feel that.'

Haq ran his hands over it too, his eyes on mine, and frowned.

I placed my hand over his, our fingers weaving together, and moved him to the spot in question. 'See. Can you feel that ridge and, there, that rise?'

He lifted his hand, placing it over mine, and slid it over the curved belly of stone.

'And here too.'

He raised his brows, questioning.

'They're witness marks, Haq. Signs of hands at work.'

'And so?'

'Well, I believe every part of the cooking process feeds into the final dish. Even the utensils. And perhaps it's possible, just possible, that some part of the person who crafted it, his intentions, hopes, dreams, finds its way into the very fabric of the work. And then in some way, into the food I prepare.' I pulled the cover over the stone. 'I bet that sounds crazy to you.' I looked away, feeling embarrassed that I'd so freely expressed such ideas.

'Wow,' he sighed. 'Do you have a clue how extraordinary you are?'

I bit my lip. Extraordinary. Not ordinary, I thought, smiling and frowning and wondering if he meant extraordinary 'special' or extraordinary 'weird'. I was surprised to find myself hoping it was the former.

At the *taka tak* restaurant, we chose a chicken dish with peppers and a lamb dish with onions and tomatoes, which ended up resembling coarse mince. We ate between laughter and chatter, sharing stories. Jen still looked glum, but had agreed to join us anyway.

Part way through the main course, a man I didn't recognise appeared by my side. The routine was becoming predictable. He was smartly dressed in a suit and tie, albeit a couple of sizes too big. He shuffled to sit beside me. As he leaned back, Haq's smirking face came into focus behind him, several seats away. I returned a momentary scowl.

This man had long, razor-sharp eyes and asked many questions about every single aspect of my life. Polite society trains us to answer questions that are put to us and I battled with this as he conducted his interrogation-style questioning. What had I studied? Where in London did I live? What did I want to make of my life? How good were my cleaning skills? And even, how committed was I to my devotional prayers? I dodged some questions, joked my way through others, but stopped dead when he asked what had gone wrong with my marriage. Without a pause, I excused myself and walked away. I seated myself beside some distant relative engaged in a heated discussion over the correct spicing of a *taka tak* dish. Having failed the interview, Curriculum Vitae Man straightened his tie and left. He was clearly not impressed.

As tea was served, Haq's fiancée Farah arrived, and oh my! She was Penelope Cruz crossed with Aishwarya Rai: sheet-silk hair, slender, seductive, the delicate features of an angel combined with fleshy kiss-me lips and, as if that wasn't enough, her willowy form tapered to breakably thin wrists and fingers. She kept casting her doe eyes longingly up at Haq, which couldn't have been easy with the weight of false eyelashes she was wearing. I felt a clench in my gut which I told myself wasn't envy, but admiration.

After Farah was seated, we persuaded Nana to continue the story of her encounter with djinn folk, which she launched back into with pleasure.

She recapped how she had been tailed by of one of the spirit folk as she entered her home when the sun was low. He'd slipped in through the door behind her, as close as her own shadow. In the evening, when her husband, my Grandpa, returned, they sat at the table and ate. My Grandpa was different that evening. For months, he had been too busy and distracted to pay her any attention and had become neglectful of her. He stayed away some nights, leaving for lengthy business trips, which would be upsetting for any recently married bride. That evening, though, he became attentive, noticing for the first time since their wedding her extraordinary beauty. This pleased Nana and that night was like her wedding night. That was all she was going to say about that. She didn't want her husband to leave for work in the morning, so intense had their connection been, but being a loyal worker, he ate his breakfast and left.

After he'd left, Nana remembered the black cat she'd let into the house the day before and went to look for it. She couldn't find it, so decided the cat must have slipped out when her husband left for work. But when she checked, she found both of the doors bolted . . . from the inside. How therefore had her husband left? She began to shout for him. Perhaps he hadn't gone after all. Feeling confused, as you can imagine, she ran to a neighbour. That's when she discovered that her husband had been in an accident and had spent the previous night in hospital.

She returned home in tears, so confused. She couldn't understand. Who had she slept with the night before if it wasn't her husband? She ran about the house, checking the windows and doors were locked, then wrapped herself in a blanket and hid under the bed. Just then, the cat appeared playing with a paper ball, kicking it about the room. She watched it from afar, peeping from the wrap she'd hidden in. That was when she saw. The cat kicked the paper ball away and something kicked it back. Something invisible. And then the cat looked up at empty air, as if there was someone there. My Nana ran from the house to her father's without pausing for a breath.

Her husband was in hospital for two whole months, but it only took two weeks before my Nana discovered she was pregnant. If the child had been conceived on the night of the visitation, it would be no ordinary pregnancy and no ordinary child could be birthed from such a union. If it had been a visitation by a djinn, then my Nana knew what to expect, for there are many tales of unions between djinn and human and the offspring they bring forth. There would be visible signs that the child was born of the union of two such different creations of God. A djinn baby doesn't have the feet of human babies at birth; they appear reversed. And when such a baby is born, it can walk straight away. It is said to be a most fearful thing to observe.

Nana cried endlessly and prayed relentlessly. She even arranged several complete readings of the Holy Book to ward off the possibility of the birth of such an offspring. But she knew her husband's appetite, or lack of it. And she could do the sums. The child must have been conceived the night of her husband's accident. Nine months later, labour pains began. Intense and punishing.

At this point my Nana stopped dead.

'So, what happened? Was it a djinn baby?' Jen asked desperately.

Nana tapped her nose. 'I will tell you later.'

'This is amazing, Nana,' I said. 'I wonder why Dad didn't tell me any of these stories before he died.'

Everyone fell silent. A shift, like a change in the weather, darkened the room, Nana and Uncle Musa glancing at each other before looking down, despondent. I hadn't meant to upset them or cut the evening short.

But it didn't matter. Because shortly afterwards, my whole world would change.

The following day, Haq came over for the meal I had offered to cook for him. Uncle Musa, Nana and Aunty Gulu were very excited, as this was the first time I was cooking in Lahore. The dish, Calm-Making Cauliflower (page 47) is truly one of my all-time favourites, because the flavour when correctly prepared is simply magic. What a boost, both calming and uplifting at the same time. And when this magic alights on the taste buds and enters the body, it cannot fail to pass a deep, meditative calm into every fibre of your being. And through the calm, the mind gains a certain clarity from which decisiveness flows. There is a base of onion, garlic and garam masala (though powdered is probably better here). You fry the sliced onion and crushed garlic, brown the lamb and fry the spices, then cover with water and cook until the meat is nearly tender. Then a certain transformation occurs with the addition of the cauliflower, a good quantity of fresh tomato and a great tumble of coriander leaves at the end. The result: fresh pods of snow-white cauliflower poking through a rich, meaty, garlic-drenched lamb sauce, lifted by severely wilted tomatoes and infused throughout by large breaths of coriander, issuing the scent of freshness itself.

As Haq ate the meal with freshly baked nan bread, a deep, meditative calm, not that far off catatonic, was evident from the set of his face. I could almost see the clarity descending, not through analytical thought, but from the heavens, as the best realisations do. He sat in a reflective stupor. And my family, too, sat back in their chairs after the meal, staring at air. It was as if the calm spilled from their bodies and filled the room.

'Haq,' I said, 'was that good?'

'Oh, Addy,' was all he said before returning to private reflection.

My work here was done.

# 16

# Fast for Thought (*page 48*)

When abstinence is the only way, take:

nothing

The taste: none.
The artistry: to stay the pleasure of taste and reset the senses.
The purpose: to take a moment to do what you know you must.

AFTER BREAKFAST THE FOLLOWING DAY, I SAT DOWN with Aunty Gulu on one of the three pink sofas, a cup of thick masala tea to my right, my recording machine to my left. Aunty Gulu took the seat adjacent to me as Nana cleared the breakfast table. So began my first taped interview. I clicked the red record button. 'Can you tell me what it was like growing up here?' I asked.

She spoke of playing in the streets with her friends; the gallons of lassi (a cooling mix of yogurt and milk with nuts which they drink to survive the crippling heat); the long, lazy siestas in the stifling afternoons; neighbours, relatives, friends who would drop in; how they longed to attend weddings and Eid celebrations because then they would go shopping for new clothes and glass *chooriyan* bangles in every colour and design. She loved the way the bangles shimmered and tinkled whenever you moved.

'Tell me about my Dad when he was young,' I said next. Aunty Gulu became childlike, as she was inclined to, a finger up against her lips as if struggling with a decision.

'Mother said we have to call him Musa now.'

'What do you mean?' I asked. 'Dad's name was Ali.'

Aunty Gulu covered her mouth, released a stunted yelp and ran off.

At this point, there was no particular reason for me to be alarmed. Aunty Gulu was a simpleton and had a tendency to become confused about a great many things.

Nana, who had witnessed the exchange, came to sit with me. I asked her what Aunty Gulu meant. Nana stared at the coffee table, seemingly searching for words, and then took my hand.

'I am never wrong,' she said, modest as ever. She frowned. 'But there is something I have been wrong about, very wrong. And I am sorry,' she said, tears in her eyes. She raised her dupatta scarf to dab her cheeks and caught her breath.

I was speechless. I had never heard Nana apologise.

'Addy, *beta*.'

'What is it, Nana?'

For a beat or two, she said nothing.

'There is another reason I brought you here,' she said, her speech halting.

Another thing I'd never witnessed in Nana. Hesitation.

'Your mother was very upset,' Nana said, placing her hand upon her heart as if to muster courage. 'She didn't want to see you forever chasing after your Dad. She knew how much you loved him. And then when he left . . .'

I felt a prickly hollow form in my stomach.

'You mother, *beta*, she had terms.'

'Terms?'

'I have done a terrible thing. But I had no choice.' Nana whooped, then stifled a sob.

I was starting to become afraid. Why was Nana so upset?

'I told you a lie . . . about your Dad.'

The picture was beginning to form, even as I pushed it away. I couldn't breathe. 'Told me what?' I searched her face for more, even as I understood. 'You mean . . .'

'I had to. I couldn't leave you. Your father abandoned you. I had to stay with you . . .'

'Nana, slow down. I don't understand. Start again.' Tears began to blur my vision. Nana leaned forward to embrace me, but I pushed her away and moved to the other sofa. 'What do you mean? Tell me from the start. Slowly.'

'Addy . . .' Nana covered her mouth with her dupatta scarf and looked about the room as if searching for words.

'Tell me, Nana, tell me.'

'I lied to you. We all did,' she said, her voice breaking

as she spoke. I felt as if I was slipping down a ravine. My world diminishing, the floor beneath me shifting.

'After your Dad left, your Mum was mad. Fury like you cannot imagine. And everything I did to get your Dad to stay failed. The calls, the letters, the pleading. You remember, I even followed him to Lahore, taking you with me. I thought if he saw you, he would see what a fool he was being and return.' Nana paused to wipe tears from her eyes. 'I went to the Data Darbar every day, sometimes leaving you with your Dad, sometimes with other relatives. I cried every day, every night begging that your father return to his family. But it was no use. I could no more make him return to his family than I could make the sun rise from the West.'

She paused to take two deep breaths. 'I found peace only when I accepted my son's decision without any bitterness or resistance. Accepted him and his decision as unchangeable. A fact of life rather than something I could mould like dough. But there was a problem. After we returned to London without your Dad, your Mum's heartbreak didn't ease. Neither did her fury. In fact, she sank into a deep depression, becoming bitter and hateful. And the worst thing, the thing she could not bear, was your questions about your Dad. Where was he? When was he coming back? You were just a child, of course you would ask. You didn't understand what was going on. But your Mum couldn't bear it, the hurt he had caused you and her. Eventually, she decided she had found a solution. She decided we must tell you your Dad had died. I refused, of course. This would be a lie. A terrible lie. But she didn't see it that way. She felt it was a sort of kindness to you. A way to stop your suffering, your endless questioning. You would no longer need to face the questions that must plague any child with a parent who leaves. When I continued to refuse, she gave an ultimatum. Either your father and I agree with her plan, or I leave the house, return to Lahore and have no further part in your upbringing. It was the only way she would allow me to stay, so your father and I went along with it. And we told you your Dad was dead.' Nana looked away, covered her mouth with her dupatta and sobbed.

I could say nothing. I stared at the middle distance, my eyes unseeing. The words refusing to take meaning in my mind. 'So why tell me now?'

'*Beta*, you are big now. You don't need me. It doesn't matter if I am forced to leave any more. And now I must make amends. I had to tell you about your Dad and reunite you.'

Uncle Musa appeared at the entrance to the room, his eyes bloodshot. And I saw it then, the look in his eyes, his face, aged, but the same as those in my memories of childhood. Dad's face.

'Dad? Uncle Musa is Dad?' I said, slowly, like a child.

'Addy . . . *beta* . . .' Nana said.

'Dad didn't die?' I said, speaking to myself. I stood. The room began to sway. 'How could you?' I shouted.

'Addy,' Musa said, 'sit down, my child.' The word 'child' thickened my throat, made my breathing hard.

'We had no choice,' Nana repeated. 'I couldn't leave you and your father refused to return. There was no other way to stay with you, to raise you.' She reached for me as I stepped away. 'Stay, Addy.'

'How could you?' I screamed, backing out of the room. 'My whole life is a lie.'

I ran past Uncle Musa, or rather Dad, and pushed past Haq, who had just arrived. All my life, all those conversations, all the tears, all born from a lie. All that suffering, only to find Dad here, very much alive. I pushed at the courtyard gates and ran down the street and didn't stop. The roads rushed past me through a blur of tears. I was gasping as I sobbed like a distraught child.

Eventually, I stopped and found myself in a labyrinth of crossing alleyways, panting to find breath. It was only as my breathing slowed that I realised I was lost. Where now? I tried at first to retrace my steps but found myself buried deeper in the maze of alleyways, high walls on either side. After a few minutes, an old lady approached. She asked in Urdu if I was lost. I pushed past her. A young man appeared. 'Can we help?' he said, in accented English. I felt the rise of panic in my chest. Where was I? How was I going to get back? I didn't even know the address of Nana's family home, having been chaperoned everywhere.

'It's this way,' a voice said. My heart paused, then raced. I swung round, readying to run.

It was Haq, steadying me with an arm upon my shoulders.

Haq led me to a side street, supporting me as we walked.

'Are you okay?'

'Yes, I'm fine. How did you find me?'

'I live here, remember. It wasn't hard, you made quite the impression as you ran. But more to the point, why were you running out of the house like that? You know Lahore is a big city, and there are places you don't go. Dangerous places.'

I looked down, unable to answer for the sadness pressing at my throat, tears blurring my sight.

Haq forced a breath rapidly in and out. 'Come with me,' he said as he led me away, his arm wrapped firmly around me.

# 17

# Forgive-Me Bitter Gourd (*page 50*)

For repentance to be brought forth so that forgiveness can flow, take:

1 onion, finely sliced
3 cloves garlic, crushed
2 lemons, juice only
1 tsp red chilli powder
3 or 4 bitter gourds - sliced, salted and set aside

The taste: like a blue cheese, rich with a deeply savoury taste.

The artistry: the power to take something ugly and bitter, and raise it to high art, something utterly exceptional, truly unique.

The purpose: to promote the transformation of bitterness and hate to deep savoury love through the divine art of forgiveness. This dish is not for the faint-hearted, but then neither is the offering of a true and total pardon. It takes a big and mighty heart to let it go.

THREE DAYS LATER, HAQ WAS LEADING ME DOWN A secluded, tree-lined walkway with a high trellis above, the trees on either side trained into a canopy. Lahori sunshine dappled through the gauze of tree branches, tracing up my legs as we walked. At the end, the walkway opened to a tranquil green meadow with a small building at the centre. Unlike most areas of Lahore, it was peaceful and deserted, but for some sort of groundsman poking about. This was another mausoleum, like the Data Darbar, but for a lesser-known saint. Haq sat me on a low wall and told me to wait as he approached the groundsman, who waddled off, presumably in search of a *chai-wala*.

As I waited, a memory came. Christmas. Years ago. Dad's still with us. I must be about seven and Nana and I have cooked a magnificent *seviyan*, a creamy caramelised dessert made with vermicelli, butter, sugar and green cardamoms. I'm sitting on the floor, a tiny girl with a great oversized bowl of this milky dessert on my lap, slurping away. Dad starts asking me about what I want to be when I grow up, suggesting a doctor perhaps, or a lawyer?

My response is clear. 'I want to be a tree.'

'You want to grow trees?' Dad says. 'Work in a garden?'

'No, Daddy,' I say emphatically. 'I want to be a tree. When I grow up.'

'Oh,' he says, nodding, slow, serious. He looks to be in deep thought. 'I'm not sure we have to wait that long,' he says. And without a moment's hesitation, he stands me up, lifts my arms so they're stretched out like branches and starts to strip the Christmas tree of its decorations. Eventually, baubles hang on my ears; tinsel spins around my head, my neck, my waist; a branch of the Christmas tree is snapped off and gripped between my knees and sprinkles of pine needles are scattered randomly about me, and I am done. Effortlessly transformed into a tree, and better still, a Christmas tree.

Mum is not pleased.

I saw Haq in the distance returning with tea.

Since the revelation that Uncle Musa was my Dad, I had felt such anger about the lies that it diminished me. That first night, after being rescued by Haq, I lay still on my back in bed, staring up at the dark, seeing all those times I had spoken to Dad's image in that old, cracked photograph. I still couldn't believe he was not only alive, but in the very house I'd lived in for the last week. Before long, I fell into a shallow, fitful sleep. If Lahore had healed me, this had spun me back to darkness. I refused to speak to anyone, staying mostly in my bedroom, reading or writing notes in my Ms Mayford recipe book. Mum had called from London at least four times every day since she discovered the secret was out, but I refused to speak to her.

The second night, Dad came to my room and sat on the end of my bed. My feelings had shifted slightly. There was still anger, but now it was overlaid with a numb helplessness.

'Addy,' he said, 'I am sorry. For everything. Forgive me.'

I shifted around in bed, turning my back to him. 'I'm not ready to speak,' I said, addressing the blank wall before me. 'I'm still processing.'

'Yes, my child. I understand,' he said. 'I know I have been a terrible father. But I want to change. Make things right.'

I lay there a while with him sitting at the end of my bed.

'Tell me, Dad,' I said as I turned to him finally. But he'd already left the room, quiet as a whisper.

Haq knew everything and now I suspected he'd brought me here to talk about it. I was right.

'I just can't believe it,' I said, in response to his questioning face. I took a sip of tea. 'How could they lie to me and tell me Dad was dead? It's unforgivable.'

'It must be upsetting, I understand. But very little in life is unforgivable, really.'

I pulled at some long dried grass by the wall.

'Addy, you should try to see it from their point of view. It was unwise, unfair, but it was well intended. No one meant you any harm.'

'So you think it's okay to lie? It's okay to let a little girl think her Dad is dead, grieve him, miss him? And all the while, he's alive and well. And I'm just supposed to say, that's okay, Dad? How've you been all these years?'

There was a pause after my passionate outburst. When the silence returned, Haq said, 'Perhaps.' We sipped tea. Then Haq continued, 'I have to say, I think you are so lucky.'

I huffed.

'Hear me out,' he said. 'It's rare to see so much love in a family.'

I looked at him in disbelief. Had he gone mad?

'Well, it's very likely your Mum didn't want you to feel abandoned, the way she felt. She believed, for whatever reason, the idea of death was better, easier for you to deal with; that it would give you a new narrative about your Dad. That he didn't choose to leave, but a turn of fate took him.'

'I don't know what you mean.'

'And your Nana and your Dad. What choice did they have? Really. Your Nana's love for you was big, so big that she agreed to do anything to ensure she stayed with you.'

I pulled in a deep breath, annoyed, while at the same time realising I hadn't thought of it that way. I'd seen only the lies. My suffering. Not theirs.

'And your Dad wasn't going to spoil things for your Nana. How much he must love his mother, and you, in his own way, that he was willing to forgo any contact or communication with you so his mother could stay with you. And—'

'Don't say it,' I cut in.

'What?'

'I know what you're going to say next. That if I accept everything as it is, accept I have no power to change it anyway, then I will be happy.'

'My God. You were paying attention. I worried perhaps you thought I was talking about cookery.'

I laughed despite myself.

We stared at the long, motionless grass for a while as the sun cooled and the air became infused with reds and oranges. The empty plastic teacups had fallen on their sides, as if resting with us. After a short while, a magnificent bird with a crown of black-and-white-tipped orange feathers flew past and landed some distance away.

'What is that?' I said, stunned. Haq told me it was the hud-hud. A beautiful creature that had been personified as the wisest of all birds in a literary masterpiece he loved by Farid ud-Din Attar. In it, the birds of the world gather together in a bid to find their leader. They make a long journey crossing seven valleys.

'The second valley is the Valley of Love,' Haq said, 'and there the birds must abandon reason for the sake of love.'

As I watched him speak, I found I couldn't look away. It was as if his eyes had collected sunrays and were emitting an ethereal light of their own.

'You know, my father says the most important quality of all is forgiveness. It's one of the ninety-nine names of God, in fact: The Endlessly Forgiving, because it's his most overpowering quality.' He swept his hand over my hair, as gentle as a breeze. 'Listen,' he said, 'families make mistakes, I'm not denying that. But there's no point in staying angry, even if you have good reason to be. It won't change anything, other than to make you hard and embittered. Your family love you. Your Mum and your Nana have always been at your side. I know you will find a way to let this go. Abandon reason for the sake of love.'

This made me teary.

I lowered myself off the wall on to the grass and buried my head in my knees, deep in thought. When I lifted my head, I screamed, leaping up off the grass on to the edge of the wall. Haq took hold of me as I teetered, nearly tipping off the wall, and then started laughing at me as I pointed. On the mud was a lizard, doing a staccato zigzag towards me at lightning speed. It was the colour of raw chicken.

'That's a *chipkali*, a common house gecko. They're everywhere in Pakistan . . . you should check the walls of your bedroom at night.' Haq was laughing uncontrollably.

'What?' I said. 'It's creepy!'

'It's not that. It's just that my first thought was perhaps you do take after your Aunty Gulu after all.'

I pushed him hard with the flats of both my hands. He didn't flinch. 'Watch out, I'm going to tell that princess of a fiancée of yours that you're no good.'

This only made him laugh harder. 'You'll have to think of a better deterrent than that,' he said. His face stilled and for a moment he held my gaze.

On the way back in the rickshaw, I elbowed Haq every time I detected silent laughter in the jog of his shoulders.

That evening, Jen came knocking on my door.

'Can I come in?' she whispered. I didn't reply. She entered anyway and sat on my bed, her face stretched with concern. I had no doubt she feared I'd slipped back to that dark place which brought us here. I told her I was okay, that it was just the shock of the news, but that actually, I was beginning to see it for what it was: a good thing. She showed me a beautiful pair of sandals she'd bought that day, covered with sequins and tassels.

'They're gorgeous, Jen,' I said. 'Did I ever tell you about the time I left the house with a different shoe on each foot?'

Jen laughed. 'No,' she said, 'you daft woman. But I'm so pleased you're getting better, getting over things.' She reached over and placed her hand on my arm. 'So, tell me about the shoe thing.'

In the morning I sat on one of the pink sofas, the rising scent of heated dough, butter and sugar surrounding me. Breakfast was being prepared.

Uncle Musa, or rather Dad, appeared in the doorway, nearly tripping over when he saw me out of bed. He flattened the invisible hair at the back of his head, as always. I looked at him carefully. Every part of him. He looked so much older than the Dad I remembered. His nose was as bulbous as ever, but his hair, or what was left of it, was now just wisps of grey. He had grown frail. The skin of his face was fragile, breakable. His eyes reddened as I stared.

'Dad,' I said.

His chin trembled. 'Addy, *beti*,' he said.

'Can you take me shopping for *ladoo* sweets, as you once said you would when I was little?'

Dad couldn't speak. He sobbed like a child. I comforted him like a parent.

I had made a decision. I had to accept the fact that nothing I did, said or felt would change what had happened. The lie that I had lived with for years was what it was. And I could do nothing about it. So, I was left with two choices. Accept it, drop the anger and move on, or continue to rail against it and stay stuck. With the latter I would only be torturing myself. I had, in the cold light of day, acquired a dad, as if he'd risen from the dead. What mattered was that he was alive, here in Lahore. That fact wasn't going to change. And I would embrace it.

He said he was sorry. So sorry. And I told him that I had been deeply hurt, but was ready to talk. Nana sat in the corner of the room, moving between sobs and smiles. Dad told me he had tried to stay, make things work, but the fighting was destroying him. He couldn't be a father to me the way things were.

The tears and explanations were followed by hours of catching up, and reliving memories. Our attempts at Lego towers, the long walks, conversations on the swings, the day he made me into a tree, and the way he'd fed me by hand, even when I was big enough to feed myself. We left out memories including Mum. There were things about their relationship I knew I'd never understand. He told me he had tried to get in touch, but was racked with guilt, fearful of what Mum might do. On some level, he felt he was to blame for everything. He had, after all, chosen to leave, failed me, failed Mum. He didn't deserve to have things his way.

That night I cooked Dad my special Forgive-Me Bitter Gourd, page 50 of my cookbook. As I sliced and fried and stirred, I wished for all the bitterness between us to be gone. And that I might be capable of total forgiveness, so no memory of the hurt remained.

# 18

# Brave-Making Mulligatawny Soup (*page 51*)

For the evaporation of cowardice, to enable you to face up to what you must, take:

1 onion, finely sliced
2 cloves garlic, crushed
½ tsp red chilli
3 or 4 curry leaves
a pinch of mustard
a pinch of fenugreek seeds
4 peppercorns
salt to taste
melted butter - a great wodge of it
fried meat of your choice laced with tamarind paste

The taste: rich and meaty and strong.
The artistry: the blending of East and West.
The purpose: inspires bravery and strength, from which honesty will surely follow.

TWO DAYS AFTER OUR RECONCILIATION, DAD CAME UP with a plan. He wanted to take us to the famous Anarkali Bazaar, but first, with animated enthusiasm, he sat me down with Jen to watch his favourite movie, *Mughal-E-Azam*, which told the story of the bazaar's namesake, Anarkali. As we watched, transfixed, we ate great mounds of juicy satsumas, peeling them as we ate – a sweet, honeyed heaven. The film was a sumptuous riot of colour, music and dance, featuring the iconic Madhubala. On my bedroom wall at home, I have a beautiful picture of Audrey Hepburn, dressed in pearls, diamonds and a tiara. Had I been born and brought up in the Indian subcontinent, the poster on my wall might well have been that of Madhubala.

We set off for the bazaar at sundown, which was when life generally began here, under a Lahori skyline streaked with vibrant oranges and pinks. Haq had arrived right on time to accompany us.

Anarkali Bazaar was a force of nature. If the word 'marketplace' conjures a line of Sunday market stalls where you buy vegetables and slightly tatty clothes, you'd be very much mistaken. We were dropped at a side street and from there we entered an endless maze of stalls, the din of people everywhere and so crowded with shoppers that we had to continually squeeze past. It was a rainbow of vibrant colours, with traders selling anything from fabrics, food, clothing, to shoes, jewellery, and more. A kaleidoscope in motion. Great rivers of silk streaming from rolls; makeshift eateries where *chaat* and *chai* were served; ornate walls of jewellery, both fake and real; stalls selling a dizzying variety of *chadars*, shawls with decorative brocade and embroidery, stitched with mosaic mirrors, sequins, lace. And dotted here and there, a few ready-made clothing stalls, less popular as the cost of getting a *darzi* to tailor-make your clothing was so cheap in Lahore. Exactly the opposite to London.

'Addy, I want to buy you this,' Dad said. He held up a red, green and yellow sequinned number with a tinsel-edged scarf. The chances of me wearing it ever, I estimated to be significantly less than zero.

'It's beautiful, Dad. Thank you.'

Haq was clearly of my opinion, his smirk overlaid

with mock innocence as I tried it on, feeling remarkably like a Christmas tree.

We wandered around the stalls, hypnotised by endless unfamiliar sights, sounds and scents, stopping every few paces to touch and admire. We were lost in the carnival-like atmosphere. Jen bought a shawl; I took a while selecting an armful of glass bangles. And Dad added to my Christmas-tree outfit with a pair of Aladdin slippers that actually spiralled up to a pointy curly tip at the front.

'Thank you, Dad,' I said, slipping them deeply into my bag in the hope they might slip out the other side. By this time, Haq had his hand over his mouth, his shoulders gently jogging.

Eventually, we headed off to eat. Haq had planned for us to try the celebrated mulligatawny soup served at a nearby restaurant within a hotel.

On the way, we couldn't resist sampling some of the famous street food the bazaar had to offer. Men clasped machete-type knives between their toes and used both their hands to slice meat. This was then passed to the street cook to be thrown into giant, wok-like karahis, fed with foot-high flames over which meat, onion, garlic and spices charred and sizzled into something majestic. The air pulsated with heat and smoke and steam and the scent of exquisite herbs and spices as the transformation from raw meat to meal happened before our eyes. Dad insisted I try a particular tandoori chicken with freshly baked nan bread, soft as clouds rising endlessly from hellishly hot tandoors. We were finally on the same page regarding our preferences. It was sensational.

The crowning glory of the day was the mulligatawny soup when we finally reached the hotel restaurant, a dish which is famed throughout Lahore. Haq explained that it was actually an English soup, developed during the Raj. It was deeply soothing, rich and warm and meaty. The ingredients include a tablespoon of tamarind, red chilli, garlic, mustard and fenugreek seeds, peppercorns, salt, and curry leaves, with onions, rice and meat fried in butter ghee. This, as I had noted in my recipe book, is a soup which inspires the bravery needed to cope with life's challenges in a way nothing else can.

I will never know if it is the soup that is the source of Jen's courage that evening, or a culmination of all that came before. After finishing the meal, we all make our way to a nearby mall which sells gold and ready-made clothing. Jen and I are trying on traditional *choori dar* outfits, which consist of a dress with tight, ruched trouser leggings. I help her into hers, setting the pleats in the leggings and zipping up the dress at the back. A moment later, she's smiling as she swings the dress about in front of a cracked crooked mirror, pinned precariously on the wall of a makeshift changing-room area. She then puts the scarf on her head.

'Look, I'm Little Red Headscarf.' We giggle as she poses.

'Suits you,' I say, speaking to our reflections in the broken mirror, the crack placing each of us into separate shards. 'Jen, I haven't thanked you for everything. Bringing me here, caring for me.' I take her hand. 'You're really the best friend anyone could ever have.'

She begins to cry. I place my arm around her and hug her sideways, still looking at the two of us in the reflection. Her tears become sobs.

'Calm down, Jen. Never could take a compliment, could you?' I say, giving her a little shake.

'Addy, I'm not what you think. You should hate me.'

I turn her so she is facing me. 'Are you okay, Jen?' I ask.

'It's all my fault. That's why I wanted to bring you here. To make it better. Put things right.' Her sobs morph to wails. She can hardly form words between gasps and splutters.

'What the matter, Jen? I don't understand.'

'All my fault.' She becomes inconsolable, hyperventilating as she backs further into the changing area, still decked out in ornate Pakistani attire. I cannot understand her, but in between the sobs I finally hear the word 'Gabe'. My stomach becomes heavy, hollow.

Our gazes meet for a moment and then part. I see it then, the guilt in her eyes.

The world shifts even as I stand motionless. Is she saying what I think? Have I been so blind? I have known Jen forever, and yet she feels in this moment like a stranger. The two most important people in my life wouldn't, couldn't. Haq hears the crying and comes into the changing area, trying to calm Jen down, insisting she take a sip from an Evian bottle.

I hold a rail of clothing for support as my mind slips back to that day. The day I stepped nervously up the stairs. One step at a time. The creaking floorboard. The scent: earth, musk, saline. The whisper of cocoa butter, such a familiar scent that I somehow couldn't place. The sight of Gabe, hiding as he lay before me, naked in bed in the early evening. And then the wardrobe, my clothes tidied away. I feel sick, a retch rising in my stomach. I now see. All along it was guilt bringing Jen to sadness and tears. How could she have looked me in the eyes all this time? How did she console me as I wept? The world about me spins. I'm doubled up, dry-heaving in between the dresses on the rack.

As I gather myself, I push Haq aside from Jen. There's fury like fire in my gut. My throat is tight, my heart thudding so hard it makes my eyes jolt. 'You?'

Jen looks afraid and stands gingerly to face me.

'It was you?' I have never felt such rage before. I am out of control, grimacing, fists clenched, heat rising in my face. 'You . . . you and Gabe?' I say.

'Ads, I'm sorry, I'm . . . it just happened.'

And there it was finally. The Admission.

I am upon her. Pinning her down. 'Bitch, you bitch,' I hear myself scream as if spoken by another. Just then I am lifted away as I swipe at air, kick clothes and metal rails, push at the men who hold me back. Jen, hair dishevelled and panting, gathers herself up and runs off, instantly swallowed by the crowds.

My whole world tips and is tumbled into shapes I no longer recognise as my knees give way and I fall to the floor. As if the world mirrors my anguish, the same thing happens around me in Lahore.

A roar builds, punctuated by shouts. A rippling explosion like thunder. Screaming from afar.

Then everyone around me runs.


'What is it, what's happening?'

'I don't know, I don't know.'

Haq approaches a running man and exchanges rapid-fire words.

'*Mardia, mardia,*' the man shouts as he runs away.

'What does it mean?' I ask Dad.

'Murder,' he says. 'Murder.'

Haq corners another runner.

I wait, hunkering down under the clothing rails of the shop with Dad, both of us hiding. All around, shop-keepers leap over stalls, drag shutters down in a single move. Transactions halt part way while gathered items are dropped as people run.

'A politician has been killed,' Haq says, returning to us.

'What, who?'

'An opposition party leader's been killed while campaigning,' he says, but I cannot connect the words, make sense of things.

'Just come,' Haq shouts, pulling at my arm, and the three of us flow into the tide of runners, all making their way deeper into the mall towards the underground car park. Smashing windows, a rippling of rifle fire, the yell of marauders. We pause momentarily, back away to let a swell of people pass.

'Where's Jen?' I ask. 'Where's Jen?' My voice goes unheard against the noise. We move, tracing the edge of a wall leading to the underground car park.

'Stay here. Don't move,' Haq says. 'It's not safe. I'll find Jen.' He disappears into the crowds as the smell of smoke rises about us.

'But who are *they* and why are they doing this?' I ask Dad.

'People. They go crazy.'

I don't understand. Assassinations happen the world over, but why the rioting?

But there's no more time for questions. Haq is gone, and I hide low with Dad against a pillar. I think of Jen lost in the crowd, my feelings conflicted, confused. No-one saw which way she'd run. How is Haq going to find her in this mess of moving people? I decide I have to help and stand to leave.

'No, Addy. Stay here,' Dad insists.

'But Haq won't be able to find her on his own.'

I pull away from Dad's grip.

'Addy,' he says. Then, after a beat, 'I love you, daughter. God protect you.'

With that I run into the pulsating crowd.

I am in the underground car park and it isn't long before I realise the foolishness of my decision. I run back and forth, becoming more and more lost. I try to retrace my steps to where Haq had left me, but everywhere looks the same. I hide beside a parked car, fear rippling waves of nausea through my gut, when I hear a voice. Faint, barely there.

'Leave me alone,' it says.

Jen's voice. I run towards it and there she is, between parked cars, two men facing her. On the floor to one side, her red scarf lies mangled on the tarmac.

# 19

# Devastation-Dashing Red Rice Soup (*page 55*)

For devastation to be dashed so that it cannot make a comeback, take:

4 cloves garlic, finely sliced
2 tsps cumin seed
2 litres boiled red lentils, soupy and soft
a dash of chilli (say ½ tsp)
salt to taste
butter, a great wodge of it
basmati rice

The *taste*: lightness and flight.
The *artistry*: clarity and simplicity.
The *purpose*: to ease nerves and soothe you at times of finality or change, and instil an attitude of gratitude no matter what test may befall.

DAD, HAQ, JEN AND I WERE SITTING IN A HOTEL LOBBY with about thirty others. Haq had found us and chased away the men. He'd brought us to the safety of the nearest hotel to wait for the madness to pass, and so we took refuge in the marble-clad lobby from the disturbances outside. News reeling on the hotel TV screens told of the assassination of an opposition leader in a city some 200 kilometres away from Lahore and how this had resulted in riots across the country. Officials advised those visiting Pakistan to leave immediately, and Haq helped Jen book an earlier flight back to London with the reception staff; one of the last seats available. There was a sense of an ending in the city. The feeling echoed within me as I grappled with the discovery that all along, Jen had been the 'other' woman in Gabe's life.

I didn't know what to think of Jen, of our friendship.

I was deflated, weakened by her revelation, but equally and inexplicably strengthened. It seemed so clear that I should have guessed, that I hadn't been wrong about Gabe. The signs were all there for me to see, but they were too close. I stared at the wall of the hotel in a daze. Jen had been a vital part of my life, and now nothing would be the same again. Could I ever forgive her? And what did this mean for Gabe and me? I didn't know. It was all too much to deal with. It could take years to find answers to those questions.

Haq came to me and, leaning over, asked if I was okay.

I said I was.

'Addy, Jen told me. About her and . . .'

I looked up at him, shocked. 'She told you?'

'Everything.'

I felt searing, raw humiliation. The indignity of it all.

'Look,' Haq said. 'Do you want to talk about it?'

'No,' I said, my voice terse, raised. 'I can't cope with any preaching right now.'

Haq backed away, his breath held, nodding lightly as he returned to his seat.

Eventually the hotel sourced a taxi, one of only a few willing to be on the road at this time, and we were driven home. The taxi waited outside to drive Jen onwards. As soon as we arrived, Nana held me in her arms and wouldn't let me go, while Dad held both of us in a wide embrace. The three of us clustered as one. Nana hadn't known for a few hours whether we were safe.

Jen came downstairs, her bag packed. She paused at the door to look at me as she left. I kept my eyes on the floor. As the car pulled away, the memory of what had just passed between us reeled.

Jen is frozen, bearing the stance of a startled animal. One of the two men holds a stick. He's little more than a kid. A teenager, perhaps. He approaches Jen. I retreat, aware how close, how vulnerable I am, my instinct to save myself. He speaks to the other boy, but I don't hear what he says. They laugh. He reaches for Jen's arm, dark finger lines upon her peachy skin. Everything slows as fury rises in my blood. I step forward, find my fight. But then I see it playing in my mind. Imaginings as vivid as memories. Gabe. Jen. Their naked bodies entwined like vines beneath the sheets. Him kissing her. The visions make me gasp, breathe in as if I'm drowning, try to fill my lungs. I fall to a hunch upon the tarmac, its oily smell in my nose.

The second boy approaches Jen. I try to stand and step forward. Hesitate. *Why? Why should I?* And then a thought: through everything, Jen never walked away. Bad choices. Good choices. All her choice. And I see. In spite of what she's done, she's stayed with me. And I know as I watch the one who's holding her, it isn't what she's done, but who I've become. Who would I be if I stand and watch? And with that, I stride towards the men. Savage rage burning in my gut. Fury. Jen runs to me. I step between the men and Jen, hands fisted at my side. They lose their nerve and back away. Then Haq comes running towards us.

My phone hadn't had a signal over the last few hours, but now that I was home, it jolted back to life. A text popped up. I held my breath when I read it. *Call me urgently. Can't get through.*

I brought up the number to call, but then the phone rang in my hand, Gabe's name lighting up the screen.

'Hello,' I said, weakly. 'Gabe? My God, is that you?' I paused to steady my breathing. 'You called?'

'Ads, finally. I've been trying to reach you for ages. Are you okay?'

I couldn't speak for the shock, my heartbeat erratic. He had materialised finally, like an apparition, after all these weeks. It was so strange to hear his voice and it filled me with joy. I pictured him in his academic tweeds, looking every bit the young professor he hoped to become. How many times had I dreamed he would call me back, that he would return to me so that I could feel his comforting presence once again? In my dreams, when he appeared, I'd imagine everything was as it was before.

There would be no need for words of explanation. No 'sorry', 'if only', 'why'.

'I've been calling since I heard about the trouble in Lahore, but the network was down. You are okay, aren't you?'

I didn't respond for a few seconds. Then, 'Yes, I'm okay. I don't know what to say, Gabe. I've been desperate to hear from you.'

There was a pause. His voice softened. 'I got your letter, Addy.' He sighed. 'Look, Ads, I have to speak to you.'

I could tell he was nervous. I pictured his grand, angular hands, slipping in and out of his pockets, sweeping through his hair. 'Now is fine, Gabe.' I hesitated. 'It's so good to hear your voice and—'

'No. Please, Addy. Let me speak first.' He took a deep breath.

I steadied myself, pressing my back up against the wall.

'I got your letter a couple of weeks ago. I didn't reply and . . . and I'm sorry for that. I'm sorry I never contacted you all this time, since . . . I can't imagine what I've put you through.'

I allowed the pause that followed, picturing what it would feel like if he were here, looking into my eyes right now.

'I've been such a fool. I've been an idiot.'

I said nothing.

'Are you okay?'

'I can't really say,' I said. 'I don't know what to think any more.'

'Ads, let me get to the point. Your letter . . . I want you back too. I'm sorry about everything. Look . . .'

'Yes,' I said, without pausing for a beat.

'I want you back, Squid. I do.'

I stood for a while, Gabe's words circling my mind. Words I had yearned to hear for so long, words I'd imagined would right my world. I had begged the universe for these words. Prayed for them at the Data Darbar, petitioned God at every opportunity. And now, here they were. The words I'd longed to hear being spoken in my ear.

And yet now everything had changed.

I huffed out a half laugh, taking a private moment to enjoy the irony. 'Gabe, you've always said there was no-one else?' I said.

'There's only ever been you.'

'You must have thought me mad, suspecting you.'

'I love you. That's all that matters.'

'So there really wasn't another woman?'

'I already said, Addy. No. I couldn't do that to you.' There was a pause. Just the sound of our breathing on the phone.

'So, nothing happened with Jen?'

Silence.

Haq appeared at the entrance to the sitting room. He raised his hand, but seeing I was on the phone, went through to the kitchen.

'How . . .'

'She told me.'

He pulled in a deep breath. Released it in a slow stream. 'Squid . . . I was going to tell you.'

I flinched. 'Don't call me that.'

'I'm sorry. About Jen. It just happened, and—'

'Just happened?' I cut in. 'That's your explanation? See, I might need a little help here. On how something like that *just happens*?'

'Addy, don't do this. I wasn't thinking. And it was only the one time, after that news from the clinic. I . . . I know how that sounds, but . . .' He paused, taking a few forced deep breaths. 'Look, I have been such an utter, total imbecile.'

'Yes,' I said. 'Yes, you have.'

'But I want you back, Squid. I do.'

'No,' I said.

For a while there was silence.

'I agree,' I continued, 'perhaps you are an imbecile. And, just to be clear, all evidence points to the fact you are. Or we could call you an idiot, a dullard, or a moron if you want, because it's all semantics. You gave it all up, Gabe. Gave me up.'

'Alright, alright . . .' he said, a hint of irritation in his tone. 'Ads, I'm back now, and—'

I cut in. 'And even if it's true,' I carried on, 'that you are a complete imbecile, how does that make all of this okay? And how would I ever know if something else isn't going to "just happen"?'

I looked around at the room, examined the red rug, the coffee table, the pink sofas, then paced to my left, thoughts coursing through my mind. I thought of Nana. Mum. I thought of my Uncle Musa, my Dad. The Dad I had mourned over so many years, the Dad I'd had endless imaginary conversations with. And I thought of Jen.

'No. You are something quite different. You are the kind of person that thinks nothing of lying, for one thing.'

'Addy—'

'One who willingly cheats—'

'Wait, wait Addy—' Our voices overlapping.

'. . . and deceives—'

'Come on—'

'. . . with my best friend,' I said, my voice raised to eclipse his.

Then silence again.

'Please,' he whispered, diminished.

'Hmm,' I mused to the coffee table. 'It's not the act,' I said, still addressing the table, 'but everything it means.'

I turned, imagining I was face to face with him. 'Gabe Anders,' I said in the style of a barristerial cross examination, surprised by the robustness of my tone. 'I've got you back. But I don't want you. And you don't deserve me.'

Later, I sat alone.

People often go to their 'happy place' at testing times. A place in their mind where waves break against sand, perhaps, where sunshine makes scatter patterns upon whitewashed walls and there's the scent of freshly cut grass in the air. I had always known my happy place. It was a taste and a meal my Nana first cooked me many years back. I could smell cumin seed and sliced garlic frying in butter with a dash of oil. I pictured the texture and colour, and my mouth watered at the thought. I knew it would engulf my senses with its rich, alluring tones and that the slightest taste of it in the smallest measure would bring me relief. The dish I needed: *Devastation-Dashing Red Rice Soup*, page 55 of *MS MAYFORD'S RECIPES TO CHANGE YOUR LIFE*.

This dish is the embodiment of everything that is soothing, being a broth and yet so much more. It is flavoursome, rich and warm and along with the accompaniments, also provides variety to the tongue in both texture and taste. It eases feelings of finality and loss. This may sound like hyperbole, but it isn't. Its introduction in my Ms Mayford recipe book reads as follows.

There are many times when we're in need of emotional support, a crutch or simply the love and comfort of a good friend. Especially when there is an impending sense of finality, a sense of an ending. For such times, you need Devastation-Dashing Red Rice Soup.

You wash the red lentils and place them in plenty of water to boil, adding a dash of chilli, a little salt and one minced clove of garlic. You fry a further three cloves of garlic, sliced into random, disparate shapes, in butter with a little clutch of cumin seeds. When they've turned golden and the butter is frothy, you pour it into the watery lentils. It must be served upon basmati rice - only basmati - and served in a deep bowl with the essential accompaniments of lime or garlic pickle (shop-bought is fine) and finely sliced red onions over which have been trickled some lemon juice and a dash of salt.

I was jolted out of my thoughts when Nana came into the living room and called me to eat. The dish she'd prepared already set on the table: Devastation-Dashing Red Rice Soup.

She sat down next to me. 'So, it was Gabe on the phone, wasn't it?' she asked, frowning. 'What did he want?'

'Oh, nothing, Nana, nothing at all,' I said.

'You are okay?'

'I'm fine, Nana.' And I was. Really, I was. Possibly better than I'd ever been.

Nana eyed me suspiciously as she served the red rice soup.

'Oh, and Haq came for you,' she said as she closed her mouth over a spoonful of the soup. 'I told him you were on the phone to your husband in London.'

# 20

## It's All Good Lamb and Taro Root (*page 59*)

For lessons to be learned and for stories to let loose their truths, take:

6 chunks of lamb, on the bone
8-10 taro roots, peeled and chopped into halves
1 onion
4 garlic cloves
2cm/1in ginger
1 tsp garam masala powder
1 tsp chilli powder
3 tomatoes

The taste: the taste of peace and love. Utterly phenomenal.
The artistry: to receive the unexpected when you least expect it. Taro root being a fruit of fertility from which endless possibilities abound.
The purpose: acceptance. Know that everything is just as it should be. And that all hurts are lessons in disguise, come to make us grow.

IT WAS THE DAY BEFORE WE WERE TO LEAVE FOR LONDON. Nana was coming back with me, but I knew that soon enough she would return to Lahore to be with her family here, for good.

A couple of days after the riots, Lahore began to settle and my mood shifted. Seeing Gabe in a new light was the elixir I needed. The truth brought relief, but there was much to process and I knew it would take time. I called Mum to make up, to tell her I knew about Dad and that it was all okay. In the meantime, life chugged on. We returned to eating copious amounts of fruit and delicious meals. The best part was that I had the time to get to know Dad better. After a week, when things were largely back to normal, he took me to many new places in Lahore, like Shalimar Gardens, Minar-e-Pakistan, Liberty Market, famous restaurants, and some lesser-known sights, such as a village famed for its buffalo milk tea.

I thought about Jen, and sometimes about Gabe. But mostly I thought about Haq. I missed him. Since he had visited while I was on the phone to Gabe, he hadn't been back, and that was over a week ago. Had I offended him at the hotel on the day of the riots? I wondered. Or was it something to do with my call with Gabe? I felt guilty about missing him. He was, after all, engaged to be married, and in fact the most likely reason for his absence was that this was the week of his nikah marriage registry. He had told me he and Farah wanted the ceremony to be a private family affair, given that the three further days would consist of dazzling celebrations, involving hundreds of guests.

But even with Nana, Dad and Aunty Gulu around, there was an emptiness without Haq. Something missing. I wanted to tell him about the places Dad took me, wanted his penetrating gaze. I decided I would try to see him or at least speak to him before I returned to the UK the next day. Say goodbye. Wish him all the best.

Today, Nana and I would be making It's All Good Lamb and Taro Root, our final meal before leaving for London the next day. It was the perfect goodbye meal and the epitome of comfort and taste as well as magical outcomes. My Ms Mayford entry for this dish reads as follows:

For total pleasure, this dish must be eaten with your hands. Tasted first with your fingertips before it reaches your mouth. You will be fooled into thinking that what you see in the gravy is a potato, but taro root cannot be compared. A taro root is to a potato what a cheese is to a mouthful of sand. It is creamier than cream, lusher than lush. You must crush the taro root with the pressure of fingertips upon a freshly cooked roti, still hot, scalding even. Press firmly and it will resist. Keep going and then it gives. It doesn't crush, crumble or dissolve. It slides apart, thick and smooth, like nothing you've ever felt before.

As you prepare the meal, remember to wish as you work, to voice your intention, for this is the most important ingredient of all. When you bind your hopes and dreams into the thick of the mix, You Will See Wonders!

As Nana and I cooked, I thought about the past weeks, months and years. I remembered what Nana would say – 'Addy, nothing that hits you was ever going to miss you. Nothing that misses you was ever going to hit you' – and how this had been a source of comfort for me. A couple of nights earlier, I'd pulled out my Ms Mayford recipe book as I watched the ebb and sway of a candle flame.

Life has set me on fire (I wrote). It has kneaded me, salted me, heated, burned and roasted me. It has pieced me, peeled me, turned and sauteed me. And I have been transformed, just as the ingredients in my recipes are, into something better. My disparate parts melded. How ironic that I had to journey thousands of miles from home to find my way back to myself.

I didn't have all the answers, but one thing was clear. I had made a decision to love every part of my life. The past, present and future. The good and the bad. I would reject regret. It was a pointless and torturous emotion anyway. I would not carry the lead weight of disappointment on my shoulders either. From now, I would hold acceptance in the same place as I held desire.

If my mixed heritage and multi-faith upbringing had done anything for me, they had given me a gift. The ability to hold two opposing ideas in my mind without judgement, without feeling the need to choose. I had been handed a toolkit in which I kept different ways of seeing the world, and the ability to see the beauty and value of each in any situation. And Haq had helped me see this, shown me the wisdom of it. The power of connection, of being open equally to the familiar and unfamiliar. When I returned to London, I planned to join a cookery school and pursue my dreams without compromise. I would embrace all that I am, every part of me. And I would no longer fear the judgement of others.

As the meal was nearing completion, I could hardly believe it when I heard Nana welcoming another family at the front door. It sounded like an older couple accompanied by a young man, presumably their son, being led into the living room. She was relentless.

Nana as ever became engaged in an animated conversation with the mother and my stomach sank at the thought of yet another 'introduction', but I went in to greet them regardless. It was only as I turned into the living room that I realised it was Haq's mother who was speaking to Nana, with Holy Man and Haq looking on. I was so relieved that I would see him again before leaving for London. I leaned to look behind him, expecting to see Farah, as he had promised to bring her here after the nikah registry. But she wasn't with them. We gathered on the pink sofas and Aunty Gulu brought tea. Haq was dressed in a suit, so I assumed because he was back at work now that the ceremony was over. He sat next to me, beaming a great smile.

As the elders talked, I took my chance. 'Haq, I'm so glad you came. I wanted to thank you for everything . . . you know, like saving my life,' I said, a note of sarcasm in my voice. He laughed. 'But seriously, you disappeared on me.' My eyes filled as I cast them over to Dad, sipping tea and conversing with Holy Man. 'So, what's happening?' I said to distract from the tears. 'You going somewhere?' I gestured to his suit.

'Yes,' he said. 'Here, to see you.' His voice was jovial, but his face was intense, motionless.

'You know, I thought when I heard your mother that this was another *rishta* meeting – Nana introducing me to yet another suitor,' I said, laughing.

Haq didn't laugh; his face grew soft. 'What makes you think it isn't?' he said, running his hand down his tie.

My stomach flipped. 'But what about . . .'

'Calm-Making Cauliflower,' was all he said, nodding and smiling a one-sided grin.

I could hardly breathe. 'So, you're not . . .'

'No.'

My heart raced as we drank tea, caught up on the drama of recent days. Nana kept casting her sharp eyes over, looking between me and Haq during her own lively conversation. When she caught my eye, she cocked her eyebrows at me.

This time, I smiled and with the slightest dip of my head, nodded. Nana beamed.

We all sat around the dining table as Aunty Gulu served the It's All Good Lamb and Taro Root. As we were eating, Haq leaned into Nana.

'Nana,' he said, 'you never told us the end of your djinn story. What happened to you?'

'Yes, Nana,' I said. 'Did you have that baby?'

Nana looked nervously to her right and then left, then leaned in. 'Yes, I had the child,' she said in a whisper.

'Oh my God,' I said, mirroring her hushed voice. 'What was the baby like? Did it have strange feet? Was it a djinn baby?'

Just then, Aunty Gulu walked in with some fresh nan bread, and Nana, with wide eyes, cocked her head in her direction and clucked.

'No!' I said.

'Yes,' Nana said.

'No!' Haq said.

'Yes, yes,' Nana said.

Haq dipped his head, his shoulders jerking with silent laughter. He looked at me, his piercing eyes luminous with blues and greens, and winked. We ate the delicious lamb and taro root, all of us positively swimming in a sublime sea of rich, meaty creaminess. As the plates were cleared, Nana called us back over to the pink sofas. Tea was served.

'Now,' she said in the manner of an announcement, standing proud in front of us, 'I want to talk about these two.' She swept her arm to where Haq and I sat, addressing Holy Man and his wife. 'Don't you think they are well matched? What a beautiful couple they would make.'

The elders nodded to each other as if we weren't present.

'And I don't believe in long engagements,' Nana added, winking.

I could feel my cheeks burning, a creeping shyness, as if I were aged ten again. Haq leaned in to me.

'Shall we get out of here?' he said. 'It's getting a little claustrophobic.' He scanned the elders, and the coffee table (for a brief moment only), and then looked at me with those eyes, smiling his winning smile.

I pulled in a deep breath. 'Yes,' I said. 'Yes. Yes. Yes!'

# Acknowledgements

I am ever grateful to my dear mother and grandmother who expressed their love through the meals they cooked. Without their mind-blowing dishes, this book would not exist.

Thanks also to my amazing agents Jon Elek and Millie Hoskins for their constant encouragement and guidance in both the good times and the tough ones. Your belief in me is inspiring and I am deeply grateful to you and your colleagues at United Agents.

I feel privileged to have been chosen by the immensely talented team at Headline with Mari Evans and Imogen Taylor, and am especially grateful to my brilliant editor Amy Perkins, who is both wonderful and wise. I am in awe of your unrelenting focus, eagle eye and your uncanny ability to know my mind better than I do.

Gratitude to my fellow students at Cambridge

University and my tutors, especially Midge Gillies and Elizabeth Speller, as well as the many fellow authors who have imparted their wisdom and feedback over the years.

Finally, thanks to Zak and Haris, my miracle boys and the best and most consistent distraction in the world. And to you, Kam, for understanding my passion for story. Without your endless support, my publishing (and so many other) dreams could never have come true.

# Recipes

If you found your mouth watering as you read
*To Lahore, With Love*, read on for Hina Belitz's
full recipes for three of the most delicious dishes,
so that you can cook like Addy in your own kitchen.

# Commitment Cake

This is an all-time favourite in our home. Its divine taste is derived from the combination of orange blossom water and caramelised sugar syrup.

## Ingredients
500g medium semolina
225g golden caster sugar
275g salted butter, melted
300g Greek yogurt
1 tbsp baking powder
Dried rose petals/mint leaves to garnish (optional)

*For the sugar syrup/attar*:
180g golden caster sugar
120ml water
Juice of 1 lemon
2 tbsp of orange blossom water

## Method
1. Preheat the oven to 200C/450F/Gas 7.
2. Place the semolina and sugar in a bowl and mix together. Add the melted butter and combine. Make sure the semolina and sugar mix is completely coated by the melted butter.
3. Mix the yogurt and baking powder together in a bowl. The mixture will bubble and expand. Stir this into the semolina and mix well.
4. Tip the mix into a medium baking dish and gently spread.
5. Bake for 35–45 minutes until the cake has browned on top and a skewer inserted into the centre comes out clean.
6. During this time, prepare the sugar syrup. Place the sugar and water in a pan over a high heat. When hot, let it simmer for about 10 minutes. The syrup should very slightly darken and reduce. When a little syrupy, remove from the heat and mix in the lemon juice and orange blossom water.

7. Drizzle most of the sugar syrup over the surface of the cake while it is still hot and leave it to soak in. I don't like to flood the cake too much, so I leave a small jug of the sugar syrup to one side so that more can be added according to individual taste when it is served. It is great to have bites both with and without the syrup to appreciate the full breadth of flavour this cake offers.

8. Dried rose petals (or mint leaves) can be scattered over the cake for decorative effect.

(Adapted from Joudie Kalla's cake Namoura in *Palestine on a Plate*)

# Lose Your Rage Chicken Korma

This is a sublime dish with a mouth-watering and distinctive flavour which I have enjoyed all my life (I even have photographs of me tucking into this meal as a toddler).

### Ingredients
1kg chicken thigh or breast (thigh is best, but breast also works. If thigh, the chicken should be chopped into 6/8 pieces. If breast, the chicken should be cut into chunks of approximately 3 cm).
1 large or 2 medium sized onions, finely sliced
6 cloves of garlic, peeled and sliced
Olive oil and 1 tbsp butter
1–2 tsp red chilli powder (according to taste)
4 tbsp or 250g Greek yogurt
2 tbsp coriander seed powder
1–2 tsp salt

*Whole spices*
2 black cardamoms
1 tsp of whole black peppercorns (6–8)
½ tsp of whole cloves (3–4)
1 tsp of cumin seeds
2–4 cm cinnamon stick

### Method
1. Fry the onions in the butter and a generous amount of olive oil, enough to just cover the onions. When soft, add the garlic and fry until golden brown.
2. Add the chicken and briefly fry to seal.
3. Add the salt, chilli powder, whole spices, coriander seed powder and fry briefly.
4. Add the yogurt and allow it to boil on a high heat. Keep stirring. Continue to cook the mixture in this way for between 5–6 minutes. If it dries up too much or starts to stick to the base of the pan, add 1–2 tbsp of water. It is done when the oil begins to separate and become visible.

5. Add water until the chicken is nearly fully covered, mix thoroughly and bring to the boil. Then reduce the heat level and let it cook at a simmer for 15/20 minutes or until the chicken is cooked. (Thigh meat will need longer than breast). More boiling water can be added if needed as it is cooking. I like to keep the sauce thin, though I know others like it thicker.

6. Serve on basmati rice with plenty of sauce or nan bread.

# Make it Better Tea Rice

This is a fragrant and refreshing rice with subtle savoury and sweet notes. This dish is delicious served hot or cold, either with another dish, or on its own with a little yogurt as an accompaniment.

## Ingredients
350g basmati rice and approx. 650ml water
1 tin chickpeas, drained
1 onion, finely sliced
5 cloves garlic, minced
250g plain yogurt (or 4 tbsp)
2 tsp salt
Olive oil

*Whole spices*
2 black cardamoms
4 green cardamoms
1 tsp of whole black peppercorns (6-8)
½ tsp of whole cloves (3-4)
1 tsp of cumin seeds
4–6 cm cinnamon stick

## Method
1. Fry the onions in a generous amount of olive oil (so the onions are just covered), until softened, then add the garlic. Fry for a further 2/3 of minutes until the onions turn golden brown.
2. Add the chickpeas, salt, yogurt, whole spices and fry for 4-5 minutes. When properly melded together, take some of the water set aside for cooking the rice and bring to the boil. Like a teabag, the whole spices steep in the water and release their flavours. You can actually leave the mixture for a while at this point if you wish, as the spices continue to flavour the mix.
3. Add the rice and the water. The liquid should be about double the volume of the rice. Bring to the boil then reduce to simmer until the rice is cooked. Depending on the type of rice, you may need to add a little more water to ensure the rice is fully cooked.